The love of danger . . .

Saxon's Pentagon staff officer days were history. He'd be planning and executing Force One's hostage rescue mission and counterterrorist death strike. But first he looked forward to returning to the Big Mean One's fenced-off compound at Camp Lejeune to work out the tactical framework of the presidentially mandated assault.

This would in all probability be the most ambitious hostage rescue mission in the history of special warfare. In many ways, it would be more ambitious than the classic 1973 Israeli rescue mission at Entebbe Airport in Uganda.

The mission soon to be undertaken by Saxon's Marines would, as a matter of course, also be the most dangerous and most difficult special operation in combat history as well.

So why, Saxon asked himself, was he so damn happy?

USMC

A Novel of the Marine Corps

DAVID ALEXANDER

J

JOVE BOOKS, NEW YORK

THE BERKLEY PUBLISHING GROUP
Published by the Penguin Group
Penguin Group (USA) Inc.
375 Hudson Street, New York, New York 10014, USA
Penguin Group (Canada), 90 Eglinton Avenue East, Suite 700, Toronto, Ontario M4P 2Y3, Canada
(a division of Pearson Penguin Canada Inc.)
Penguin Books Ltd., 80 Strand, London WC2R 0RL, England
Penguin Group Ireland, 25 St. Stephen's Green, Dublin 2, Ireland (a division of Penguin Books Ltd.)
Penguin Group (Australia), 250 Camberwell Road, Camberwell, Victoria 3124, Australia
(a division of Pearson Australia Group Pty. Ltd.)
Penguin Books India Pvt. Ltd., 11 Community Centre, Panchsheel Park, New Delhi—110 017, India
Penguin Group (NZ), Cnr. Airborne and Rosedale Roads, Albany, Auckland 1310, New Zealand
(a division of Pearson New Zealand Ltd.)
Penguin Books (South Africa) (Pty.) Ltd., 24 Sturdee Avenue, Rosebank, Johannesburg 2196, South Africa

Penguin Books Ltd., Registered Offices: 80 Strand, London WC2R 0RL, England

This is a work of fiction. Names, characters, places, and incidents either are the product of the author's imagination or are used fictitiously, and any resemblance to actual persons, living or dead, business establishments, events, or locales is entirely coincidental. The publisher does not have any control over and does not assume any responsibility for author or third-party websites or their content.

USMC

A Jove Book / published by arrangement with the author

PRINTING HISTORY
Jove mass-market edition / February 2007

Copyright © 2007 by David Alexander.
Cover design by Steven Ferlauto.
Text design by Kristin del Rosario.

ISBN: 978-0-515-14256-3

JOVE®
Jove Books are published by The Berkley Publishing Group,
a division of Penguin Group (USA) Inc.,
375 Hudson Street, New York, New York 10014.
JOVE is a registered trademark of Penguin Group (USA) Inc.
The "J" design is a trademark belonging to Penguin Group (USA) Inc.

PRINTED IN THE UNITED STATES OF AMERICA

10 9 8 7 6 5 4 3 2 1

AUTHOR'S NOTE

Some place names and descriptions of locales, weaponry, and military procedures have been modified where necessary to suit the requirements of the narrative.

Though it stands on its own merits, this book was originally titled *To the Shores of Tripoli*. It concludes the story begun in *From the Halls of Montezuma*, which precedes it in the saga of Marine Force One.

—D.A.

From the Halls of Montezuma,
To the shores of Tripoli,
We fight our country's battles
In the air, on land, and sea. . . .

If the army and the navy
Ever look on Heaven's scenes,
They will find the streets are guarded
By United States Marines.

—from "The Marine Hymn"

BOOK ONE

Weapons of Choice

Terrorists will do absolutely anything to create fear. The fact that they attack innocent men, women, and children doesn't cause them a second thought. If they could do more harm, they would.

In Iraq, the improvised explosive device is the terrorists' weapon of choice. But if they could get bigger devices or get their hands on chemical, biological, nuclear, or radiological devices, they would use them.

—Air Force General Richard B. Myers,
speaking at a Pentagon press briefing
in March 2005

1.

A FRESH START

SAXON'S PERFECTLY TIMED SPINNING YOKO-GERI pounded the heavy bag with a force equal to a blow from a sledgehammer. Heads turned even in a place as jaded as the Pentagon gym as the force of the Isshin-ryu karate snap kick threatened to tear the 150-pound bag loose from its heavy chains and send it flying across the acrylic-surfaced wood floor.

Saxon spun full circle and faced the bag in a combat stance, raining down punishing hand and arm blows, going at the punching bag like it was his worst enemy come to life. Saxon was surprised by his anger; like some caged animal inside him, it had reared up and lashed out savagely at its keeper. Saxon socked the heavy bag another time for good measure; now he understood the sudden burst of frenzy. The caged beast inside Saxon was Saxon himself, and the cage he was in was an office and a desk on the Pentagon E-Ring. Today the door to that cage was open and, after long months of confinement amid the greatest bureaucracy on earth, Marine Force One's commander would finally be set free again.

It had been five miserable months since Saxon's orders to report for staff duty rotation had been cut and sent down from the office of the Marine commandant. Five months of hard labor behind a desk behind the walls of what to Saxon was the largest prison in the world, condemned to do time among the biggest ass-kissers in the military, business, and politics.

In combat a soldier knew where he stood. In the field it was do or die, right and wrong, no in-between. In the world of the Puzzle Palace somebody always had your ass up against the wall, only most of the time you didn't know it until it was too late and your ass was broken.

Fortunately, the president's phone call had changed everything for him.

The word had come down from the White House.

"Get Colonel Saxon," the president had ordered.

Now Marine Force One had a mission again, and Saxon was to ramrod it.

The terrorist hijacking of a cruise liner at sea was a disaster for many but a blessing in disguise for Saxon and Marine Force One. Another week, another morning of carpooling through the rolling West Virginia countryside, another slice of tasteless mall pizza, another meeting with a dark-suited idiot from DARPA touting some new superhelmet that would never grace the head of anything but a dummy on a mock-up battlefield, another empty night of screwing some office secretary he'd met at a bar in Arlington or Alexandria . . . another minute of this bullshit and Saxon would have lost it.

But he hadn't. The call of duty from the White House had changed it.

Saxon gave the bag one more swift, hard karate foot blow for auld lang syne and broke for the shower. Then it was out into the Pentagon's mazelike corridors.

The corridors had been arranged like spokes on a wheel. The plan had been to construct a building that was easy to navigate, but you needed musclepower to get around—the Pentagon had originally been built without elevators, and the main form of locomotion, even today, was the standard-issue pair of Mark-I human feet.

The A-Ring, Corridor 3 of Wedge 3, was more lightly trafficked at 9:35 A.M. than it would be by noon, but the activity level was still high by ordinary standards.

The Pentagon never slept, not even on weekends. There was always business being transacted, always people moving around, and a dark custom-tailored suit and power tie made up a uniform often more commonly visible at the building than any other kind.

The Pentagon probably had more dark pinstripe suits and smarmy rep ties passing through its corridors on any given day than might be found at a convention of Hong Kong tailors. Civilians ran the show here. A soldier learned that quickly and never forgot it. The Defense Department had the choicest offices, located on the building's top floor, and most of the big shots were White House appointees. The prime real estate on the E-Ring went with the territory.

Saxon's destination was an office on the C-Ring, Corridor 1 of Wedge 2. Yoda's lair on an ice planet. It belonged to Marine Force One's Pentagon liaison and founder, General "Patient K." Kullimore.

Kullimore's civilian secretary, a woman who'd been at the post for a long time, sent him right in. Saxon had come here often during the past several months, and her boss had told her he was one of the few who

----

enjoyed the privilege of unhindered access to the general's presence.

"Your last day," Kullimore said as Saxon entered Patient K.'s office. "How've you held up?"

"As well as possible."

"Got some medicine for you."

Kullimore held up a mint.

"Sure, General," Saxon said.

He pretended that it wasn't sour beyond endurance as he sucked on it.

Kullimore ordered coffee, brought in by a Marine orderly. Privileges of rank, Saxon told himself. Kullimore got out a bottle of brandy. He poured each one of them a shot into the coffee. More privileges of rank.

"Actually, this is the medicine. You'll have another mint when you leave. Helps with the breath."

"Affirmative, sir. That's one order I won't disobey."

"Well, I suppose I should be grateful for at least one, Dave."

Patient K. wasn't smiling when he said that, Saxon noticed. Judging discretion to be the better part of valor, Saxon took a sip of the hot, spirit-laced coffee.

"So tell me why I'm here, General. Aside from getting your blessings on my new assignment, that is."

"Colonel," Kullimore began, "you've made some enemies. But you've also got some strong supporters.

I'm one of them. Obviously so is the president. I suppose what I want to say to you now is that my support will continue to be unstinting. I've spoken with the president. He's backing Marine Force One straight down the line. You'll get anything you need. A blank check."

Kullimore set the mug down on the general's desk.

"What's your preliminary assessment?"

The general took a Macanudo cigar from a leather-clad cedar humidor on his desk and lit up the cigar.

He gestured for Saxon to help himself. Saxon didn't. When he'd quit smoking long ago he'd quit unconditionally.

Saxon thought for a moment before he answered Patient K.'s question.

"Sir, I see it like this," he began.

IF A CROW FLEW OUT THE WINDOW OF KULLIMORE'S C-Ring office, zigged up at a ninety-degree angle through the light well that separated it from D-Ring, and then flew due east for about twenty-two hundred miles, that crow might eventually find itself perched on the deck of the *King Albert III*, a 951-foot hijacked

----

ocean liner carrying more than two thousand hostages
that was the subject of Saxon's next words.

What our hypothetical seabird would encounter
aboard the *KA III* would not be pretty, nor would the
view be especially clear, since it would be one seen
by the pallid light of a quarter moon casting its pow-
dery white glimmer across the upper deck of the
four-story luxury cruise vessel.

Here terrorist sentries in black fatigues walked
their perimeters from bow to stern, submachine guns
ported at their hips. The subguns were carried with
their safeties off, fire-select switches on full auto.
The sentries were prepared to shoot on sight, without
warning or provocation.

To the patrols, the darkness of the night meant
little, since each wore a lightweight tactical head-
mounted display that, among other things, endowed
the terrorists with false color aperture night vision,
simulating normal daylight optical conditions.

The hard men behind the NVGs, many re-
cruited from the decimated specialist ranks of failed
governments—such as the Iraqi *mukhabarat*, or intelligence service, and the *sediqqi* or special forces units
of a miscellany of now defunct Mideast nations, had
licenses to kill. Any unauthorized persons—which for

all intents and purposes meant anybody at all other than their fellow hijackers—were to be blown away on sight and the bodies dumped in the drink.

Not that there was much chance of this happening—those passengers and crew who had survived the initial phases of the terrorist seajack were now either locked in their rooms or confined to the barred cages of a makeshift brig that the terrorists had set up belowdecks in the ship's vast cargo hold. A total lockdown of the cruise liner was now in force.

At the moment the *KA III*'s position was about eight hundred nautical miles off the coast of the tiny Atlantic Ocean island of Angra do Heroismo, an uncongenial knob of rock pointing like Poseidon's upturned middle finger at the westernmost edge of the Azores.

The stretch of North Atlantic waters through which the cruise liner steamed was vast, but the ship itself was as large as an Iowa cow town. It was easy to track via overhead imaging platforms, such as Improved Crystal, a KH-14 Keyhole-class photointelligence satellite that had been jockeyed out of its regular geostationary orbit over Southwest Asia to better keep an eye on the hijacked vessel.

What the near-real-time imagery couldn't show intelligence analysts and government policymakers at the Pentagon, White House, CIA, NSA, and else-where was what was taking place inside the cruise ship's spacious hull, but for the moment what the U.S. observers had to work with was the best that could be hoped for under the circumstances.

Given enough time, the picture would become clearer. In and around Washington, D.C., they hoped that time was not running out.

CARLOS EVANGELISTA, KNOWN AS THE EVANGELIST, was beginning to have misgivings about victimiz-ing the woman. Not misgivings concerning the acts of degradation to which he'd subjected her, but to whether she was enjoying them a little too much. The terror chieftain's object in debauching the woman was, after all, to derive pleasurable gratification from the suffering his acts caused her. At first he'd be-lieved that this was what was actually taking place.

Little by little, though, the Evangelist was becom-ing more and more convinced that this *putana con las pelas rubias*, this blond bitch, was not only enjoying what the terrorist did to her but was manipulating him into doing more of it.

And he could not help himself; this was the most sobering knowledge. He had grown to savor and enjoy the taste of this she-bitch far too much. He could not stop himself. He saw this now, and realized that it might be too late. The acts he committed were becoming obsessive.

"More," the woman rasped. Her voice was a terrible thing to hear, a cross between a shriek and a moan. "Push it. Like before."

The Evangelist looked down at the woman. Her body was tied up with ropes. The veins of her neck bulged like smaller, bluer ropes.

"Bitch," he grunted. "Dirty bitch."

"Yes, more," she panted. "Harder and more."

In a fit of anger the Evangelist reached for the leather shoulder holster that was draped over a nearby chair. He had to use both hands to draw the semiautomatic pistol, one to hold the holster, the other to grasp the gun butt.

"I am going to kill you."

"Do it. I want it."

"I will. I am not bluffing, *gringa*."

His fingers tightened around the trigger at the same moment there was another tightening below, on the other thing that resembled the finger and that men in his village had referred to as a finger, in colloquial Colombian Spanish. The Evangelist felt the irresistible tightening at both levels and soon there came a bright flash before his eyes as the gun suddenly and irrevocably went off.

But when he opened his eyes again it was this lower gun, this gun of flesh, that had fired, not the deadly thing of cold blue steel. This other weapon had dropped from his hands, and he now lay panting across the back of the woman, feeling the sweat of her ass against his loins. He knew that he needed to kill her, now, as he had killed her lover in the first hours of the hijacking. The woman was a danger to him, and what was a danger to the Evangelist must die.

There was a knock at the cabin door.

"Excuse me, *jefe*, but you are wanted below," a voice said timidly from the corridor outside.

The terrorist chieftain untangled himself from this *pelas rubias* bitch. He picked up his dropped pistol from the carpeted floor of the stateroom suite.

Too bad he still needed this woman, he thought. He did, however. She had a purpose to serve later on, and then Evangelista would grant the woman her fondest wish. He had but this single consolation right now. As soon as she was of no more use to him, she would get it between the eyes.

Evangelista flashed on how he would do it. He swore the sharks would finish the fancy carving job that his knife would begin.

* * *

DOWN IN THE HOLD YOU COULD ACTUALLY HEAR THE sound of the chilly water running beneath the hull. It was at the same time terrifying and strangely exhilarating, like looking down the cold, steel barrel of a loaded pistol pointed straight at the spot between your eyes. The stowaway had taken to going down there.

He would lie down on his belly, turn his head to one side, and place his ear flat against the chillingly cold steel of the keel bottom.

He would hear the unmistakable rush of the water and the knowledge that only a mere three inches of steel separated the rest of the ship from millions of cubic feet of ice-cold ocean water that would rush through any hole and quickly swamp the ship until it sank to the bottom.

Would this be the way it worked out? What should he do? He was alone. Alone against how many he couldn't tell. He had skills, but would they be enough to defy and prevail against the might of sheer numbers? It didn't look good. He thought of giving himself up, but the thought of the cost of such an action was sobering.

He didn't hold that idea very long. Nor did escape seem a viable option. Not when he could hear and

feel the chill of the ocean, a chill so cold that it pene-
trated the inches of plate steel between the rim of his
ear and the swiftly rushing surface of the sea.

If he jumped, computing the angular motion of
the ship, and the distance he'd fall—at least three
stories—it would be equivalent to hitting a brick wall
at sixty miles an hour. That would splatter him, break
every bone in his body. Even if he lived, the chill
would numb him quickly and he'd drown.

For the moment, he'd continue to hide.

And plan.

THE BUILDING STRETCHED ITS MONOLITHIC PALE
gray bulk behind him as Saxon turned his head toward the massive north parking lot that faced the
Pentagon River Entrance. Like a tsunami of dazzling
white concrete, the headquarters of the U.S. Defense
Department and the vast military organization it controlled towered above him.

It was hard to believe that the entire edifice was
only actually four stories in height. As tall as the
King Albert III. Exactly as tall. For a split instant
Saxon pictured the hijacked liner as it would appear
when seen from a vantage point on another vessel on
an approach on the high seas.

Saxon sneered suddenly, his version of what other people called a smile. He was starting to see the target as an overlay, a sort of phantom or Fata Morgana hovering before his eyes. That was good. It meant his mind was working on the problem, working in the background like an organic computer.

He'd be back at the Pentagon, where Marine Force One had its command center, but no longer as a staff officer. That was history. He'd be back for the planning and execution phases of Force One's hostage rescue mission and counterterror death strike.

But first Saxon looked forward to returning to the Big Mean One's fenced-off compound at Camp Lejeune. There he could work out the strategic and tactical framework of the presidentially mandated assault on the ship.

This would in all probability be the most ambitious hostage rescue mission in the entire operational history of special warfare. More ambitious in many ways even than the 1973 Israeli rescue mission at Entebbe Airport in Uganda or the British SAS rescue mission at the Mare's Head nuclear plant in 2012, in which some two hundred hostages were being held by remnants of the old al-Qaida network.

The mission soon to be undertaken by Saxon's

Marines would as a matter of course also be the most dangerous and most difficult special operation in combat history as well.

So why, Saxon asked himself, are you so damn happy?

2.

BATTLE LINES

EARLY WINTER IN THE UPLAND PASSES OF THE northern Caucasus range presented the paradox of majestic beauty coupled with ever-present peril. The jagged mountains, glaciated at their peaks, then broadening to colossal black granite slopes and mammoth summits, were forbidding even in high summer.

In winter only fools dared the constant threat of blizzards and avalanches, and now, in the few last weeks of cold that preceded the spring thaw, this forbidding mountain country was still very solidly burdened under the depths of winter. The black sawtooth ridges seemed to rake the soft gray belly of a tired, ashen sky whose vast emptiness was relieved only by

----

the occasional passage overhead of a mountain eagle, crying out as it unavailingly scanned the barren slopes below for its truant prey.

This was not a time of year for war. Not here. It was a time instead for the peasantry who ranged these baneful highlands to slaughter their livestock and impregnate their scrawny women, to produce new seed stock to carry their vulgar race into the bleak and uncertain future that awaited their wretched kind.

The colonel general thought these thoughts as the steam from a still-hot coffee cup rose into his flared nostrils.

Foul stuff. Why did he drink it? He supposed he liked it. He supposed he also liked the chill of the gray granite boulder that he sat on, a chill that had already numbed the cheeks of his ass right through his woodland camos and was well on its way to freezing the bones of his pelvic girdle.

"Fuck it," he said aloud, in Moscow-accented Russian, "this coffee is shit," and flung the foam cup over the edge of the ridge, watching the black fluid flash listlessly for a second in the pale sunlight as the coffee hung suspended for a moment, then tumbled into the abyss.

The colonel general, whose name was Yevgeny Abramov, raised the field glasses to his face and brought the soft black rubber cups close to his steel-colored eyes, scanning across the spine of the mountain range until he focused on the shallow bowl of one of the several valleys a few hundred feet below and about five miles distant from his vertiginous perch.

The Russian could make out wisps of smoke curling from the stone chimneys of crude buildings, cars and trucks creeping along ribboning mountain roads, the tracks of a railroad right-of-way that cut around the bends and folds of a nearby hillside and then disappeared around a bend into the dusty morning light.

The colonel general nodded as he set the binoculars down on the dirt beside him—he detested weights hanging by straps from the neck—and two-fingered a Maxim filter-tip cigarette from the crumpled soft pack that lay nestled inside his weatherproof field jacket.

The army lighter was in the pocket of the jacket—metal, the old, solid kind that still used lighter fluid and flints and was windproof to boot. Soon the cigarette flared, and gray-brown smoke creamed from the veteran soldier's nostrils.

Those roads below worried him. They would support the extreme weight of heavy mechanized armor—tanks, armored personnel carriers, even fully loaded tank transporters; the engineers had made studies, they were sure. The old warrior was not as convinced as the young men who'd learned most, if not all, of their warcraft in the comfort of the military colleges of Moscow.

With a snort of derisive laughter, Abramov sucked on the sweet end of his cigarette, drawing smoke deep into his lungs.

These young shits knew nothing. How could they? They had not seen the Caucasus in 2008 or Afghanistan decades before even that.

They had not seen how the treads of T-72s that had been specially modified to withstand the rigors of mountain warfare became hopelessly mired in the mountain mud of rutted roads.

Nor had they heard the screams of dying men, helpless amid the desolate high places, as the mujahideen roasted them to death using crude gasoline bombs or blew them to smithereens with their American-supplied Dragon and TOW missiles.

Back in those last decades of the last century, it had been the old Soviet Union, led by cancer-brained old farts who were still fighting World War II, who had led the Rodina, the Motherland, into the ill-fated quagmire in Afghanistan. The new Soviet Union might yet do much the same, albeit in a new battleground.

Colonel General Abramov finished his smoke and flicked the butt end of the cigarette over the edge of the cliff to join the cold brown liquid and white poly-styrene foam cup somewhere far below.

Yes, he had been briefed on the strategic objectives and tactical implications of Operation Molotov. He had participated in the months-long series of war games that comprised both computer simulations using massively parallel number-crunchers based on Cray technology and live-fire field exercises. He had also been wired into the after-action loop, where the lessons learned in simulation could be put to the test of practicality and modified to suit real-world combat necessities by the technocrats who ran the Soviet GRU and the analysts who served them.

Yes, yes—all of that was well and good. He understood the overarching logic that drove operations in this highland combat theater. Fast, nimbly mobile Soviet forces were deployed according to the dictates of Maskirovka.

Two divisions were now encamped throughout the mountain regions of the Caucasus range, ready to deploy to their preattack positions once the Kremlin gave the order to proceed.

Yes, the mountains were only enemies if one regarded them as such; otherwise, powerful and great friends. Abramov knew the mountains for what they

----

were—not a barrier, not an obstacle, only a natural screen.

Few if any battles would actually be fought in the high, cold expanses of these granitic gargantuans. The Caucasus range was an anomaly. The range existed at the hinterland of a flat sea of high-grassed steppes rolling from horizon to horizon. The mountains were like a root of stone thrust up by accident from the mighty ranges that girdled the borders of Iran, Afghanistan, and Turkey, hundreds of kilometers south of his present position.

The actual battles of the war—using light, mobile armor and rapid-response fighting formations that would quickly roll back defenders, encircle the enemy in pincer movements, and then pulverize it to shattered junk—would all be carried out on the flat steppes far below.

The mountains were vital to the buildup stages before the attack, and afterward, as forward operational locations for staff headquarters, airfields, and the like.

Still, he had misgivings, but he would not communicate them to headquarters until he could frame them in language his superiors would understand—anything less might mean dismissal, or worse. His superiors disliked being second-guessed, liked even less being subjected to scrutiny and even ridicule from Moscow.

Abramov had seen and thought enough. He rose, stiffer for wear, from his boulder seat at the edge of the mountain precipice, and signaled toward the waiting Antonov transport helicopter that had brought him there that he was ready to leave.

At once the main rotors of the big transport helo began to revolve. The old warrior trudged toward its open side hatch, still deep in thought.

3.

A SHARK IN THE WATERS

TRIPOLI. FAR BELOW, A LINE OF BEATEN COPPER streaked the wrinkled gray-green surface of the sea in the fading brilliance of the setting sun. A shadow snaked across the surface of the waters. Its undulating form was pointed toward the Libyan capital city, now only a few score miles westward along the shifting North African coast.

That same light of the dying day fell across the brocaded, medal-festooned shoulders of the Libyan Shark as he sat by the circular window of the rotorcraft that cast its shadow upon the face of the waters.

Though he was the beholder of all he surveyed, the father colonel was pensive, his thoughts somber as the sea below. The Mil Mi-26 transport helicopter flew low above the littoral, skirting the Mediterranean coast. The pilot had been given instructions to thwart Libya's own radar system in returning its leader to the national seat of government.

Mohammad al-Sharq, known to the West as the Shark of Libya, wanted his return from the meditative seclusion of a Bedouin tent amid the desert wastes of Cyrenaica to be a complete surprise. It would both catch any startled traitors and quislings in American pay unaware, and build the growing legend that surrounded him.

Al-Sharq appeared and vanished with the suddenness and unpredictability of a whirling dervish. It served a ruler's purpose to be regarded as something more than a mere human being. What men feared most they challenged less, and a web of myth surrounding a leader could at times afford greater protection than a bulletproof vest. This is why the great kings of ancient eras cloaked their human frailties and failings beneath a lustrous veneer of self-serving infallibility, sometimes divinity.

Al-Sharq had returned from the Bedouin encampment deep within the isolation of the desert wastes to the southwest of Sirte under the baking sun of Cyrenaica, where his nomadic kinsmen had dwelled for untold ages. There he had lived as a wandering tribesman, entrusting the cares of state to his lamentably shifty underlings.

Assuredly, this was a dangerous undertaking, especially with human vipers such as Saidal Fagih and those of his stripe, but it could not be helped. Nor was al-Sharq a fool; there would be no revolt of the palace guard. Potential traitors though Fagih and his ilk might have been, they would not be stupid enough to chance failure—they were all too well aware of the consequences. Betrayal once discovered was punishable by death preceded by tortures too diabolical to be named, and a plot half hatched was tantamount to committing suicide.

The Shark of Libya knew that he could reflect for a while, if only a little while, on the sudden shifts of fortune. The neo-Soviets were treacherous. He'd known this going in, but their sudden revelation of a plan for nuclear brinkmanship was reckless in the extreme.

Only a miraculous revelation sent to the father colonel in a dream had saved him from having committed himself to a deed that would have brought untold destruction on the Libyan nation.

American retribution to an unprovoked nuclear attack on its Mediterranean carrier fleet, such as the Soviets would have had Libya commit, would have met with certain retaliation in kind. The Americans might be placid, even to the point of appearing weak, under most circumstances, but when seriously threatened they were always merciless foes who struck without remorse until, their anger finally cooled, they again grew calm and practiced forgiveness.

Al-Sharq could still almost not believe it had happened, that the Soviets had secretly armed the Berkut stealth aircraft with nuclear cruise missiles and intended to use the two planes they had provided Libya to subject the American Sixth Fleet to a tactical nuclear strike in the Gulf of Sidra.

The Americans had retasked a carrier battle group conducting littoral warfare exercises in the Mediterranean sea to challenge the Shark's proclamation of a Libyan Zone of Death.

The father colonel believed that there was little risk of a U.S. invasion of Libya. As long as he continued to stand up to Great Yankee Satan, al-Sharq figured to score a huge propaganda victory without having to fire a single shot.

Angry communiqués and diplomatic démarches would be the only ammunition he'd need to expend. He had even gone so far as to send out his two most prized military possessions—the Berkuts, the Soviet-supplied Golden Eagle advanced tactical fighter planes—on a mission to taunt the Americans and push them to the limits of their patience. That was brinkmanship aplenty for the father colonel, and he only sanctioned the Berkut combat flights because he knew that the Soviet planes were as stealthy or stealthier than anything the United States flew, including the F-22 Raptor or the F-35 Joint Strike fighter.

After the Shark's last-minute recall of the two planes, he had sat in his office, looking out across the choppy, shipping-laden gulf through the picture window.

Outwardly composed, the father colonel inwardly trembled like a leaf in the wind. He realized all too well that should the Soviets find a way to countermand the nuclear recall it would open the door to a thousand sand devils.

He fought the images of mammoth destruction that his imagination conjured with wicked sorcery upon his inward eye, willing away the gigantic mushroom clouds that careened heavenward from the heart of the battle group, casting out the far more terrifying thoughts of what American retaliation for a nuclear first strike would bring upon Libya.

The Americans had not, after all, hesitated to rain death in the form of laser-guided bombs on his predecessor, al-Qaddafi, for acts of far less belligerence.

What would they have done now in the wake of one of their flagship nuclear aircraft carriers lying broken on the muddy bottom of the gulf and a plume of radioactive effluent drifting across the Middle East? The destruction the Americans would visit on him would make the fiery annihilation of the biblical cities of Sodom and Gomorrah seem tame by comparison. Once their wrath was kindled by such an act of nuclear belligerence, no power on earth would stop the Yankee Satan from taking revenge.

Thankfully, both planes had returned safely, and their pilots placed in isolation. With the crisis over, al-Sharq had fulminated with his Soviet advisers but dared not expel them for fear of Russian military intervention—the Americans might send nuclear death, but the Russians might send something as bad or worse in the form of an armed invasion force. Libya in Russian hands was a hell scenario too frightening to even contemplate.

There matters rested as the father colonel left the Libyan capital city of Tripoli to retire to the desert emptiness of his tribal homeland in Cyrenaica to pray, to think, and to plan.

His unannounced departure had been a week ago. Now he was returning, again unannounced, as the evening sun set on another day and darkness crept across the face of the waters and the land.

The helo's sudden appearance over the palace of the Libyan Jamahiriya startled the few sojourners in the vast People's Plaza that fronted the gleaming marble building in which the leader resided and carried on the business of state. Many, having heeded the sound of evening muezzins from high-domed minarets throughout the city, were now returning to their homes and waiting harems, for the leader had decreed that all Libyan men should have many wives.

Those who witnessed the Shark's return stood and gaped as the large helicopter descended swiftly from the utterly cloudless blue sky, like a steel-bellied god plummeting into the drab affairs of mankind.

As its main rotors lost speed, the side hatch slid open and an honor guard of picked *seddiqi* leaped smartly to the cobbled paving stones of the plaza. They cradled Krinkov AKR bullpup rifles and wore green fatigues with a green beret adorned with the emblem of the desert hawk pouncing on the snake that was the emblem of the Shark's new Libya.

The green-clad *seddiqi* snapped smartly to port arms as the father colonel's personal bodyguard, dressed in custom-tailored Italian suits under which bulged the telltale outlines of automatic pistols, preceded their leader out onto the broad cobbled square.

The father colonel's close protectors fanned out through the ranks of the *seddiqi*, bullet heads on stocky necks craning this way and that, their eyes alert behind dark-lensed sunglasses as they cast about for the presence of would-be attackers, thick fingers twitching with a visible yearning to grip the trigger and squeeze out hiccuping bursts of death.

Nothing escaped the griffin stares of the Shark's trained protectors. Gesturing at one another, they signaled the all-clear, and the point man at the far end of the plaza radioed back to the Mi-26 that the leader could now safely emerge.

By this time a small crowd of spectators had gathered at the margins of the plaza. None dared to advance beyond the fringes. Their leader's protectors were well known to shoot first and ask questions afterward.

At the sight of growing, if still small, numbers of al-Sharq's fellow Libyans, pistols were unholstered and rifles brought down from port arms to hip-fire position, from which fast-cycling autorifles could rake the crowd with steel-jacketed hollow-points. They'd mow down friend and foe alike without hesitation to protect their leader's life. Not that there was any danger—the crowd was less cowed by the guns than it was awed by the appearance of their leader.

Resplendent in a dazzling white dress uniform, emblazoned with gold braid, and weighed down with medals, his polished black boots and reflective black sunglasses glittering in the late Tripolitan sun, the Shark of Libya strode majestically down the stairway of two short steps that had been pushed by flunkies beneath the Antonov's open hatch.

Hardly glancing at the gathering crowd, he promenaded purposefully toward the much higher flight of stairs—they'd been imported specially for the construction of the People's Palace from the quarries of Carrera, Italy—that led upward to the colonnaded entrance to the palatial building.

Jackbooted guards posted at the entrance showed surprise as they hastily sprang to attention, saluting smartly and clicking their heels as the leader strode past them. Attended by his armed praetorians, the Libyan Shark snapped a finger at one of his attendants. A long cheroot of fragrant Turkish tobacco appeared within the space of two heartbeats and was inserted into an ivory holder worthy of a Roosevelt, then placed almost reverently between the pursed and waiting lips of the leader.

Smoke curling over his shoulder, the Libyan

potentate strode deeper into the palace of the Libyan People's Revolution, basking in the glory of a returning conqueror.

Ignoring the imploring gestures of one of his staff who held an elevator waiting for the pleasure of his chief, the leader sprang up another flight of Carerra marble, a gleaming spiral stairwell that led to the uppermost level of the palace in which his suite of offices was located.

The Shark sensed something—he sensed blood, in fact. There was a hint—no, a stench—the unmistakable odor of treachery in the air. It permeated the rooms and corridors of the palace. The leader knew he was not mistaken. His nose for trouble had never lied before, and surely it did not lie now.

Quickening his already rapid pace, the cadence of dozens of booted feet crackling like gunfire on the stairwell, the father colonel took the last few steps at a lithe, lupine trot, barreling into the door of his offices held by a staff member far too nervous to hide the obvious guilt that showed on his face—and the shining droplets of sweat that beaded it.

Al-Sharq smiled. His smile was like that of his namesake. It was toothy and full of malice; the mask-like visage and glittering black eyes added to the impression of predatory malevolence that the Libyan colonel exuded like a miasma rising from a swamp.

Two more steps.

Three.

And then a snap of the fingers, a nod of the chiseled jaw, to signal, without words, to another palace flunky to throw open the door to the leader's office. And then another few bold strides to bring him inside its spacious confines.

To bring him face to face with the treachery that he had known from the first he would find.

"Excellency . . . I—"

"*Silence*, you who are smaller than nothing, who are shallower than a puddle of camel's urine, who are of less consequence than a puff of gas from the anus of a she-serpent who crawls the Stygian sands of Nubia."

There, seated at the leader's own desk, was none other than Saidal Fagih. Befouling and defiling the gleaming antique that his agents had purchased in London as though he had defecated all over it. Seated in a chair beside the desk was General Fedoryev, one of the chief advisers sent by the Kremlin to oversee the testing and deployment of the two gift Berkut stealth fighters the Soviets had provided the father colonel for the glory of the People's Libya.

"Excellency, please be calm. You must listen."

It was the Soviet who now spoke in place of the fear-mute Fagih, but his eyes were fastened on the slow ambit of the Libyan Caesar's gun hand as he reached for the Glock that was holstered at his hip and slid the gun menacingly clear.

"Excellency, please . . ."

But the Russian's words were drowned out by the three rapid barks of parabellum bullets exiting the muzzle of the drawn pistol in rapid-fire succession, all three of which found purchase in the polished mahogany of the desk.

The leader was a lousy shot, even at close range, but the Shark's poor aim did little to dispel the conviction in the mind of the hapless Saidal Fagih that all three rounds had found their marks in his chest. Convinced that he'd been hit and now lay dying, Fagih slid off his chair and crumpled to the floor.

The father colonel stood as though dazed for a few long moments. The smell of cooked-off cordite began to waft through the room, and shafts of sunlight coming off the hard blue desert sky outside began to describe whirling gray spokes through the thin wisps of gun smoke.

The father colonel's rage had been spent. He slid the pistol back into his holster.

"Have the desk repaired before lunch tomorrow," he ordered.

"And what of Fagih, Excellency?"

"Throw the traitorous little *mamoon*—ass-fucker— behind bars until I decide what I'll do with him."

"But Excellency, please. I can explain—" The quisling's whimperings for mercy got him nowhere.

Without waiting for a reply, the Shark of Libya spun on his stacked leather heels and exited the room like a raging lion.

He had some scheming of his own to do.

4.

BANNERS

THE PREDATOR UCAV—UNMANNED COMBAT AERIAL vehicle—soared above the clouds like a giant, tailless manta ray that had somehow discovered the secret of flight.

Predator was roughly five-eighths the size of the F-35 Joint Strike fighters flown by Marine aviation, yet unlike them, the UCAV flew its missions completely unpiloted. Nevertheless, though it was equipped to carry out certain mission functions autonomously, the UCAV was kept under positive human control at all times by secure remote microwave linkages. When the unpiloted vehicle's flight path took it around the earth's curvature, putting it out of range of radio waves, the link was maintained via the Pentagon's secure Milsat network.

Such was the case at the moment as the UCAV soared high above the dark waters of the vast ocean below at an altitude that was listed as "undisclosed" to everyone except the few names on a federal bigot list clamped tighter than a hundred-dollar bill wadded in a miser's fist.

The remotely piloted aerial vehicle was armed with a formidable array of weaponry that included two nose cannons firing .50-caliber ammunition and AIM-9L Sparrow missiles carried in an internal munitions dispenser, a kind of jukebox of destruction that stored firepower on a revolving bin.

The UCAV was also well equipped for reconnaissance and surveillance missions. The primary role it played on this high-altitude overflight was to support just this mission.

Its sensor array, clustered around the underbelly and the chined leading edges of Predator's airframe in a miscellany of hull-conformal compartments, could be modified by ground technicians to suit specific individual mission parameters.

The UCAV's present mission called for a higher ratio of photoimaging surveillance capability to weapons capability, and Predator's onboard sensor suite reflected the operational mix. The UCAV had four onboard high-resolution cameras; three were active at all times, the final one kept on standby in the event one or more of the main sensors failed.

The C^4ISR chain—Pentagon shorthand for command, control, communications, computing, intelligence, surveillance, and reconnaissance—stretched from the Predator's officially undisclosed ceiling altitude, and equally undisclosed present location high in the night skies above the Atlantic Ocean, to a restricted enclosure a single story above a darkened horseshoe-shaped control center between the third and fourth floors and C- and D-rings of the Pentagon.

A bank of video consoles, linked to high-speed, massively parallel computers, glowed in the darkness as Marine chief technical officer "Doc" Jeckyll monitored the surveillance imaging data transmitted by the UCAV thousands of miles away. The imaging was instantaneous but was technically near real time because of an imperceptible 1½-second latency due to over-the-horizon transmission via satellite. To all intents and purposes Jeckyll was viewing the intel hot off the remotely piloted vehicle's sensors.

Jeckyll, piloting the drone aircraft using a joystick and keyboard, never even noticed the minuscule lag. It wasn't much different from computer gaming, except

----

there was nothing virtual about this reality—a weapons console enabled Marine Force One's chief technical specialist to unleash industrial-strength firepower on targets in the air or on land and sea.

Sure, it was a kind of gaming, but on an entirely different level. Nintendo warfare just didn't come close to being a usefully descriptive term.

"UCAV is now over the IP, boss," Jeckyll said into the rice-grain mike at the end of a flexible boom as two confirmational beeps sounded from the computer terminal in front of him. These indicated that the UCAV's inertial navigation system had guided it to the weapon platform's initial point over the target, and confirmed the map reference by querying an orbiting global positioning system satellite.

"Everything's go on the intel."

"I copy that, Doc."

The answering voice belonged to Colonel David Saxon, who was at the other end of the comms loop. Marine Force One's CO sat in his office at the force's compound at Camp Lejeune. Hard, bright sunlight and crisp, cold mountain air streamed in through the partially open windows. The laptop on the desk in front of Saxon relayed intelligence from Jeckyll's workstation in the MF-1 command center at the Pentagon.

His face lit by an eerily colored glow, Jeckyll scanned the images flitting across the surface of the flat-panel monitor in front of him. Altitude, azimuth, mean air temperature, and other flight data were constantly updated on toolbars, one of which showed that the UCAV's altitude was now at 61,073 feet—at the edges of the rectangular image area. Low-light imagining filters enabled the photoimaging sensors to zoom in on the target with extreme precision and clarity even though it was a great distance away from them.

The target was the *King Albert III*, and Jeckyll, via Predator, was conducting RSTO in advance of the impending hostage rescue mission that the force had been ordered to plan for and execute by 0400 hours within fourteen days' time.

Subject to orders from the White House to delay or speed up the mission timetable, Marine Force One considered the mission an already accomplished fact. On his return from staff duty at the Pentagon to Lejeune, Saxon had immediately sat down at his laptop and written out the mission orders that would set all of the necessary gears into rapid motion.

One of the first things the colonel's orders had created was a high-level planning cell made up of the Big Mean One's top operational staff, and including

----

Bart "Doc" Jeckyll and Sergeants Death and Berlin
Hirsch. Saxon and his team were good to go, except
for one predictable problem—interference from the
spooks.

Like a bad apple that kept turning up, the CIA's
Rempt was again a problem dumped in Saxon's lap.
Saxon had gone to his "rabbi," General Kullimore,
but Patient K. had advised him to deal with Rempt on
his own. Kullimore was wired into every corner of the
U.S. and NATO military establishments, but Rempt
was one wire even the formidable Patient K. couldn't
pull.

"If it gets too bad, just shoot the fucker," he'd told
Saxon, sounding like he was only half joking. "The
bastard won't be missed."

"How about putting that in writing, sir?" Saxon
had asked, and soon found himself dismissed from
the general's presence.

Well, he might just wind up fragging the spook in
the end. Hell, he'd thought Rempt had bought it back
in the highlands of the cross-border Turkey–Iran region three years before. The covert black helicopter
strike had left a charred, smoldering corpse in Rempt's
stone yurt, all right, but not his, as it turned out when
Rempt reappeared among the living during the mission's closing phase in Yemen.

Whenever Rempt made an appearance there was sure to be trouble for Marine Force One. Another thing about Rempt was that Saxon had never been completely sure whose side he was actually on. Rempt sometimes seemed to score field goals for the opposition as often as for the home team.

Saxon made up his mind that this time he'd frag Rempt for sure if it came right down to the nitty-gritty. Patient K. had been right about one thing at least: if Rempt bought it, nobody would care much.

While Saxon was mulling over these thoughts, Doc Jekyll had swept the UCAV over the hijacked cruise liner and gotten a bushel basket full of good photointel in the form of full-motion video and high-resolution stills that the Marine Force One mission planning cell could use to plan and rehearse the raid on the terrorist-controlled oceangoing vessel.

There wasn't much activity on either of the ship's three decks, and the heliport just aft of the main exhaust stacks sat empty under the quarter moon. Jeckyll saw seajacker patrols walk their perimeters, and noted that the bad guys comported themselves like trained professionals instead of amateurs. That fact would be logged and would go into the decision matrix along with the rest of the data.

There were no signs of hostages at this late hour, at

least not any that were visible on any of the exposed areas of the vessel, and there was no telling what was happening belowdecks, either. That, thought Jeckyll, would be the subject of further intelligence-gathering efforts later, probably using remote robotic sensors infiltrated aboard ship.

For the moment the UCAV had done its job, and it was time for it to return to the arsenal ship *George Kennan*, which lay at anchor about five hundred nautical miles to the south, not far west of the Cape Verde Islands.

The *Kennan*—crammed to the gills with supplies, spares, and gear of every description—had been tasked by the navy to serve as Marine Force One's seabase for the mission's duration. Low-observable, yet fast and equipped to accommodate VSTOL aircraft such as the V-22 Ospreys and F-35 JSFs flown by Marine aviation, the *Kennan* would serve as Force One's forward operational location and main jump-off point for the impending hostage rescue and counterterror mission.

At 0412 hours GMT, two MF-1 technical specialists stationed on the deck of the *Kennan* heard the sound of jet turbines from somewhere high overhead. The turbine scream got louder, then became a deafening shriek, as a dark shape suddenly plunged from the heavily clouded nocturnal skies and made a silk-smooth three-wheels-down landing on the deck.

The techs produced portable digital instrument packs as they approached the large, black, hawklike visitor and began snapping open ports on its fuselage. Marine Force One's robotic black eagle was back in its steel-plate nest, bearing in its beak a few choice sprigs from a far-off place.

GENERAL VLADIMIR BULGANIN STILL GLOWED WITH the flush of pride that had warmed his blood since he had received his orders personally from the general secretary himself. He was conscious of having been selected above the heads of older and far more seasoned veterans for a mission of vital importance to the Motherland.

What a change from only a few hours ago, when having first received instructions to appear before the general secretary, he'd been stunned and afraid.

Surely this meant trouble, and big trouble, too, he'd suspected. True, his orders had made no mention of any wrongdoing, and Bulganin had no idea what he might have done to invite punishment. Yet what other explanation could there be? It seemed unlikely that a summons of this kind might mean anything else.

The vast relief he'd felt when it turned out that a promotion from colonel general to full general status, rather than a court-martial and firing squad, awaited him was overwhelming, and it took every bit of Bulganin's self-control to avoid showing such unbefitting emotionalism.

The general secretary gave no sign of sensing the astonishment and discomfiture of the young soldier, although the neo-Soviet leader's eyes, which missed nothing, took in the obvious signs of the younger man imposing self-control.

So he'd thought it was the end of him? the NSU chief executive mused privately. *He'd believed I'd summoned him to meet his doom. Would my own reasoning have been as flawed as his, had I received such a summons at this time in my career?*

Then the general secretary reflected that indeed, that's exactly what had happened: he had received precisely such a summons while still a young officer.

Hadn't his predecessor, Vladimir Putin, anointed him with what Russians figuratively called "the Crown of Monomakh"? Hadn't Putin bestowed the honor of choosing him to be his successor above Malenkovich, Ostrov, Zilmanyev, and the other pretenders?

Yes, it had been he and not the other contenders

who had been brought forward into the light and the power to be crowned as leader-to-be. And no, the general secretary had not misread the implications of his own summons to the inner circle of Soviet leadership. He had understood the summons to be what it was from the first—a blessing instead of a curse, a great promotion to power instead of a descent into the maelstrom of disgrace.

But he was different, far different from the rest. That's why he led and others followed. Bulganin was exceptional, but still one of the lesser men who took orders from those born to lead.

When the time came, the general secretary would bestow the Crown of Monomakh on another, younger head, but it would not be that of Bulganin.

He had his role to play, and he'd been selected above others with more experience because he had shown initiative where those others had not. Beyond this, the general secretary considered the whelp as just another tool to be used as he saw fit, to bring greater glory to the Motherland and to himself personally.

But the general secretary said none of this to young Bulganin. He kept his thoughts to himself and masked them with a tactical smile.

Instead he shook Bulganin's hand, pinned another star on his shoulder boards, and sent him from his office with a fresh set of orders.

Those orders were to take the newly minted general to the North African republic of Libya, and to the shores of Tripoli. There, Bulganin was to command a regimental force whose orders were to seize control of the Libyan capital with or without the cooperation of its strongman, the father colonel, Mohammad al-Sharq.

There would be no time for delay, not even time to pack a duffel bag. An Antonov long-range transport aircraft already sat on the tarmac at a military airstrip eighteen miles northwest of Moscow within a secure section of Sheremetyevo International Airport. Its engines were warmed up, with extra fuel stored in long-range conformal wing tanks, and its crew had the flight plan to Libya programmed into the plane's onboard navigation system, as well as full clearances for takeoff and preference through the air corridors of Greater Russia and Eastern Europe, down through the Transcaucasus and Transoxiana, and over Iran through to the northern shores of the African desert.

Minutes after his departure from the Kremlin, Bulganin was being whisked toward the airstrip inside a spanking new Zil limousine flying the fluttering banner of the Office of the General Secretary while his newly assigned horse handler, a Colonel Davidovich, briefed his new CO more fully on the imminent operation.

Though he said nothing of his inner reservations, Davidovich did not at all like his recent assignment. This Bulganin smacked of the pompous ass—that much was painfully obvious even at first blush to the seasoned veteran. He was full of himself, and this wasn't merely repugnant to a career soldier like Davidovich, who had pulled his own weight and risen through the ranks by virtue of his soldiering. It was a dangerous trait in a commanding officer under any circumstances.

From hard experience Davidovich had learned as an article of military faith that pompous asses were bad leaders and made a great many hazardous mistakes.

Worse yet, it was too late for Davidovich to put in for a transfer. The mission was on a fast track, and the first of the many transports that was to turn Tripoli into a Russian fortress on the Mediterranean was awaiting orders to take off.

Colonel Davidovich swallowed his pride, as well

as his better judgment, and continued to brief his new commanding officer, but as the limo sped through the outskirts of Moscow, he had a sinking feeling in his stomach that wouldn't go away.

5.

FIRE AND WATER

AS THE SUN ROSE ON THE VAST EMPTINESS OF THE western Atlantic, a fast military helicopter skirted the gray-green ocean. To thwart surveillance, the turbine-assisted rotorcraft skimmed low above the sea to duck under the radar curtains of Portugal, Spain, and British-controlled Gibraltar, all of which were known to fly AWACS whose airborne and terrain radars could look sideways out to three-hundred-mile distances.

Such radars would still get a skin paint on the chopper, but hopefully it would vanish amid the surface clutter of reflected microwaves clashing as they bounced off the sea and effectively become invisible.

Inside the chopper was the terrorist mercenary who now went by the name of O'Finnegan. Inside the bubble cockpit of the chopper O'Finnegan permitted his lean hawk's face the rare pleasure of a smile.

He had just seen something amusing on the deck of the vessel below. It was his old comrade Carlos Evangelista, engaging in a bit of sport with some of his gringo captives. The terrorist chieftain was up early on the ship's miniature golf course—a raised circular platform aft of the bow, which was over-looked by the large, semicircular windows of the Old Salt, one of the ship's three restaurants.

The Evangelist was an amusing fellow, thought O'Finnegan as the chopper set down on the *KA III*'s helipad and he exited the rotary-winged aircraft, ducking low beneath the spinning main rotor blades and feeling the prop wash whipping at his fatigue jacket, holding his trademark black beret close to the top of his close-cropped head. O'Finnegan hoped that the games he'd seen the Evangelist playing had just begun rather than ended—he hankered to join in if he could.

As it turned out, the games had just begun.

The sound of an explosion told him this, and so did the dying echo of human screams, swiftly carried away on the frigid sea winds of early morning.

The Evangelist was just perfecting his golf swing as O'Finnegan neared his position on the cruise liner's seventeen-hole putting green.

Carlos Evangelista greeted his guest with a broad, amiable grin of welcome.

"It's good you've come, my old friend," he announced in fond greeting. "You have arrived just in time for the game."

"I had hoped so."

The newcomer beamed and looked around, taking everything in.

"Yes, it's not all work, you know," Evangelista told him, eyeing the arc of the glittering club end of the five-iron he was swiping back and forth across the golf ball set on a plastic tee on the AstroTurf at his combat-booted feet.

"We must relax. Refresh our spirits. The struggle will have to wait."

"Who are these good people?" asked the newcomer.

O'Finnegan meant by this the four hostages who were trussed up like hogs ready for slaughter and tied to wooden stakes at compass points on the circular golf course.

Their eyes were wide with horror but their lips had been sealed with thick strips of cloth masking tape, and they were unable to cry out. Each of the four hostages also had an olive drab satchel about twelve inches square strapped to their torso, the kind used for military demolition munitions commonly known as satchel charges.

"Ah, you mean my esteemed guests today." The Evangelist hefted the club and gestured around him with it like a circus ringmaster pointing a whip at a trained bear.

"Yes, these Americans you see are exploiters, *amigo mío*," Evangelista said. "Exploiters of their fellow human beings. They have been singled out for special treatment. You will see and be glad."

"Who are they, exactly?" the newcomer called over his shoulder as, lighting a Bull Durham cigarette of Colombian marijuana, he walked to the circle's perimeter to inspect the captives more closely.

"What crimes have they committed?"

"You see this one?"

Evangelista pointed his golf club at a man in a dark business suit and red power tie.

"He wears the toga of the new Rome. He is one of those who sits on corporate boards. A dealmaker. A boss. A capitalist."

"I see. He exploits *los pobrecitos*, the poor ones."

"Yes. And the vile proceeds of his wretched greed bought him a large stateroom suite with a balcony view of the sea. He'd even had the temerity to bring his own whore aboard. I have taken her for myself. You may have her if you wish. She did not live up to her promise, in my eyes."

"I would like that, *mi compañero*," O'Finnegan remarked, inhaling deeply of the rich marijuana smoke that helped fill his mind with visions of what this woman would be like to possess.

"Send her to me, I will try her out. But what of these others?"

"The woman."

Evangelista jabbed the stick to the left.

"Old, yet she bleaches her hair. Skinny, yet she consumes more food in one day than many a starving *campesino* does in a month. Have you heard of the Hamptons, compadre?"

"Yes. *Los Hamptons*. This one lives there?"

"In a mansion, yes," the Evangelist told the newcomer.

"What paid for this mansion? Slavery paid for it. Slavery of exploited *cholos* in South America who stitch the stinking clothes her company sells to rich American women."

"And the others?"

"Here, *el gordo*, the fat one, do you see him, *hermano mío*? He speculates in real estate. He buys the houses of the poor for practically nothing. Then he exploits poor workers to fix up the crumbling wrecks. And then he sells those homes again for many times what he first paid. This *puerco gordo* has made millions upon millions this way."

The newcomer finished his cigarette, then stepped up to the final hostage.

"What of her? Wait! I know this one."

"I would not be surprised. She has made many Hollywood movies, this *putana flaca*. And she has fucked behind the camera and she has fucked in front of the camera and she has fucked everywhere in between.

"Not fucked honestly, *compadre*, as even the little whores of Bogotá or Medellín or even Cali fuck, but she has fucked with a lecherous evil."

"They are pigs, all of them."

He spat on the AstroTurf.

"Yes, these hostages serve no purpose. They are fit for nothing. They perform no useful work. But they will provide much pleasure, much amusement. I will show you. Watch, *mi hermano*. Watch this. Wait and see what happens."

With that the Evangelist made a few more practice swipes with his golf club, then with a perfectly executed swing worthy of Jack Nicklaus, thwacked the ball into space. It took off like a big, round, white

----

bullet. O'Finnegan watched it zoom through the air and hit the business executive.

BUHH-LAMMM!

Mr. Two-Piece Suit exploded like an old bullfrog with a firecracker up its ass. There wasn't even that much blood and gore, most of it was vaporized by the explosion. As the cordite smoke cleared, all that was left of the exec was half a body. He'd been vaporized clear down to the belt line. Then the legs buckled and the mutilated cadaver sagged to its knees and listed forward, dumping guts onto the AstroTurf.

"I see. Trembler mines. *Clever.*"

"Yes, mercury switches. Very sensitive. But the secret is also napalm. A small canister is wired to the C4 charge in each satchel. The napalm burns away the flesh and bone. It's all very clean. A swift death. More than these *puercos* deserve."

"My compliments."

"Care to try your hand?"

O'Finnegan shrugged and said he'd love to try one swing. Evangelista handed his guest the golf club. The newcomer took a few practice swipes and teed off, but the ball fell shy of the mark.

"Try again."

"I am new to this game."

"Yes, it is of no shame, *amigo*. We know this.

Please try your best. Use your wrist, it is the secret of success at this."

"Yes, I have heard it said. I will do better now. Watch, you will see."

"I am rooting for you, my friend. Do not despair. You will perform well, I'm certain."

O'Finnegan tried another ball. It, too, failed to score. The newcomer took it all with good grace. The Evangelist shouted his encouragement and bid his guest try again. The ship's guest terrorist placed another ball on the cue and sized up the distance to the target.

He took a few practice swipes and then went for broke. The five iron hit the ball on the sweet spot with a dull thwack and sent it streaking through space like a small white comet.

Even before it hit, O'Finnegan knew that this shot would score a bull's-eye, which it did a second later as the ball's impact detonated the trembler mine strapped to the millionaire fashion mogul and took her legs off at the thighs in a blinding flash of incandescence that made the guest terrorist shield his eyes from the intense detonation flash.

"Bravo, *amigo mío. Bravisimo bravo, hermano mío.*"

The Evangelist clapped his hands. O'Finnegan

made a slight bow and handed his host the golf club. Then he stepped back as the Evangelist sank the next two, and final, explosive holes in one.

O'Finnegan refrained from checking his watch. Fun was fun, after all, but he'd come all this way from his island hideout in the Caribbean on very important business.

It was a type of business that would make these explosions look like children's fireworks by comparison.

BOOK TWO
Tactical-Level Decisions

Special operators are independent thinkers who are routinely expected to make tactical-level decisions during the execution of sensitive and dangerous missions, which can have strategic impacts. These attributes also make them highly valuable to the civilian world.

—A senior enlisted adviser for the U.S. Special
Operations Command speaking before
a congressional committee

6.

HARD NUMBERS

AS THE FIRST AIRLIFT OF ANTONOV HEAVY HAULERS
cleared Bulgarian airspace at forty thousand feet and
began to cross Thessalonika and Istanbul high above
the Dardanelles, invisible trip wires began to send
warning signals to intelligence agencies in Western
Europe and the United States.

Observation aircraft and ELINT (electronic intelligence) planes were scrambled from nearby NATO
bases, such as the U.S. air base at Messina, Italy.
These airborne assets and observation satellites higher
up in the envelope, combined with computer analysis
of all communications intercepts, indicated that the

Antonovs were shuttling Russian troops and war matériel to Libya.

Further surveillance of neo-Soviet military air bases in Russia showing more heavy troop haulers being loaded for takeoff all but confirmed the analysis. There was now little doubt that the NSU was engaged in a fast military grab for territory and power of a kind that had been seen several times since the end of the Second World War.

Hasty sessions at war cabinets in Western capitals—such as an emergency session of the National Security Council in the cramped NSC meeting room beneath the White House—were convened long before the first of the Antonovs touched down for landing at Uqba-bin-Nafi military air base a few miles outside of metropolitan Tripoli.

In attendance were Ross Conejo, National Security adviser to the president, who chaired the meeting; Deputy Secretary of Defense Hodding Costner; CIA Deputy Director of Intelligence Paul Marsh; and Deputy Chairman of the Joint Chiefs of Staff, Air Force General Chauncy W. Grigson.

These cabinet-level principles were assisted by a contingent of more junior staff and their aides who, occupying the rows of chairs that were lined up

USMC

---

against two of the rear walls of the meeting chamber, were known as "backseaters."

The meeting, which was convened at 0600 hours Washington, D.C., time, broke up some two hours later with a list of unofficial recommendations to the Oval Office. The text, once approved, was hand-carried up to the president by the NSA, who first briefed the vice president on the NSC's findings.

By this time—shortly after 0830 hours—President Travis Claymore had already had break-fast and his daily morning Swedish massage in the sunlit Yellow Oval Room in the West Wing—he had pinched part of the right ulnar nerve playing tennis at Camp David a few weekends before, and the massage helped with the chronic shoulder and elbow pain.

The president was sipping aromatic black Kona coffee poured by an aide from a silver thermal carafe as the NSC representatives filed in to brief him. The aide, an efficient and courteous Marine corporal, came back in a few minutes pushing a steel cart with service for four people and a salver of cold orange juice for non-coffee drinkers.

By this time the president and his Oval Office vis-itors were seated in the two black leather Italian sofas ranged on either side of a Venetian glass-topped coffee table.

National security adviser Ross Conejo glanced at the hastily scrawled minutes of the emergency session on the yellow legal pad propped on his crooked right knee as he gently set the base of the china coffee cup on the glass surface of the table. He'd taken the perfunctory sip out of courtesy, but as was his habit, would let the coffee cool to room temperature in the cup without touching another drop.

Conejo framed the main points of the meeting in his mind and then laid them before the president as concisely as possible. The National Security Council had identified three main issues that its members felt were essential to military deconfliction and withdrawal, followed by political resolution of the mounting global crisis.

The first concerned how to react to the flights of Antonov transport planes that had now been confirmed to be airlifting Soviet troops and equipment into Libya on a massive scale. Of course, the Soviets had been advising al-Sharq for about two years, but they'd always kept a low profile while the Libyans held the spotlight.

This new, uncharacteristic development by the Kremlin was something else again and indicated a disturbing new shift in global priorities for the NSU leadership. It undoubtedly meant a military buildup that would soon pose a significant threat to U.S. and Western regional interests.

Point number two concerned the linkage between this new international development and the intelligence assessments concerning the very disturbing neo-Sov buildup that had been observed in previous weeks in the southern Caucasus. Despite the Kremlin's efforts to disguise the positioning of troops and the stockpiling of strategic war supplies by the use of *maskirovka* deception strategies, Western intelligence agencies had already developed a fairly clear picture of what was actually happening and what, in reality, Soviet intentions were.

The State Department had already sent a strongly worded démarche to Moscow demanding to be informed of the Soviets' intentions in the region and reminding them that defense treaties regional powers had signed with the United States, Canada, and Europe made regional conflict almost inevitable if the Russian military buildup continued.

The neo-Sov ambassador, summoned to the office of Secretary of State Bernadette Hoffmeister, glibly denied that any military situation that might threaten the United States was now in the offing.

Even when confronted with photographic imagery showing the day-by-day growth of military stockpiles, the Soviet ambassador denied that anything other than field exercises were taking place. Hoffmeister had sent him back to the Soviet embassy with a warning that the United States and its allies would not hesitate to honor its regional defense commitments should the Soviets launch military attacks in the Transcaucasus.

Finally, point three dealt with how these two preceding matters related to and connected with the continuing hostage crisis on the high seas in which American nationals were being held captive by what were apparently well-equipped terrorists who had carried out a seemingly well-planned and successful operation.

So far the terrorists hadn't issued any proclamations or made any demands, and were merely grandstanding, but that in itself wasn't all that unusual. It fit the pattern of twenty-first-century terrorism, whose purpose, since the attacks of September 11, 2001, and Strike Day of October 6, years later, had been, as one of its late-twentieth-century theoreticians had written, "to terrorize."

The new face of global terrorism was one that always arrived masked. It wasn't open to negotiation or even to reason. It emerged like a violent storm, left havoc in its wake, and then went underground again.

Its purpose was to destabilize the world order, to blow away the underpinnings of civilization, ultimately leaving only a hollow shell that could be easily demolished with a viciously swift hammer blow. Twenty-first-century terrorism was like a cancer, eating away at civilization, and to combat it required not talk but direct, often extreme, action.

The president had already seen to it that provisions were made for the terrorists to be attacked and destroyed on the high seas by Marine Force One. As he pondered the other aspects of the morning full of cares, he made it a point to ask after the status of the Marine special forces operations group that had been preparing to stage a counterstrike against the hijacked cruise liner.

The president was reassured about one thing at least by the national security adviser: Marine Force One was holding to its timetable. Whenever the president gave the order to proceed, the hard-charging troops of Force One would be good to launch their mission.

THE PRESIDENT'S TROUBLED MORNING OF DECISION-making in the wake of disturbing international developments would have been even more difficult had he been able to read the mind of Marine Force One's CO.

Colonel David Saxon didn't share his commander in chief's optimism for a successful counterhijacking mission. The Big Mean One's commander arrived at MF-1's sea-based command center via Pave Low helicopter from the Bosa naval base on the Italian island of Sardinia. The B-52F he'd hitched a ride on from Andrews AFB had deposited him there after too many hours of listening to air force pukes talk about how great they were. Maybe they were great, but they weren't Marines, so what did it matter?

Force One's command center was in a specially sequestered section in the cavernous hold of the *George F. Kennan*, a roll-on-roll-off (RORO) ship, of a type sometimes called a sea train.

While RORO vessels were most commonly deployed for long-range shipment of military vehicles, ammunition, POL, food stocks, and the like, the enormous size of such a vessel's hold made it ideal as a kind of floating version of the MF-1 compound at Lejeune and the unit's NMCC command center combined.

Aboard ship, Saxon's Marines had access to virtually anything they would likely need to go into regional action anywhere in the world, from Bradleys to Sea Cobra attack helicopters. MF-1's sea base equipped it to respond to any contingency with rapidity and precision striking power, bar none. It was a self-contained, mobile war-fighting center without equivalent in any military organization in the world, including the United States.

Marine MPs attached to the force stood guard around the clock to make sure that no unauthorized personnel entered the secured area where the Force One planning cell was headquartered. The rest of the *Kennan*'s vast hold contained the war-fighting gear needed to equip Marine Force One for the growing list of military operations that the go-anywhere, do-anything rapid-deployment force would be called upon to undertake.

Gleaming dully under the strips of overhead fluorescent panels were ranks of armored personnel carriers, Stryker fast-attack vehicles bristling with rocket launchers and heavy machine guns, Bradley armored infantry vehicles, Abrams main battle tanks, and enough HUMVEEs to equip a car dealership in Terre Haute for a year's worth of sales. There were also stockpiles of small arms, spares, and miscellaneous gear necessary to wage high-mobility operations in a variety of fast-changing and highly mobile combat scenarios.

Sure, the hardware was the best now that Marine Force One had received the commander in chief's blessing by way of a presidential finding that specifically ordered MF-1 to act as the spear point of U.S. regional forces.

Thanks to the White House, the locks were finally off the doors. Saxon had been able to write his own ticket on this one.

Just the same, hardware alone didn't cut it, never would. The main mission that Marine Force One had been ordered to execute was probably the most difficult one it had been called on to perform in the roughly six years of its existence.

The force had been ordered to rescue the hostages from the control of the terrorists who had taken over the *King Albert III*, and to accomplish the mission with the absolute minimum loss of life to those under the guns of the terrorists. This requirement alone meant that Saxon's strike teams would be walking an operational tightrope while he as CO negotiated a political line that could easily drop him ass over teakettle into a world of bullshit.

Flawless hostage extractions were only a little harder to execute than cutting out a malignant cancer without damaging the bodily host.

In short, it couldn't be done.

No matter how careful, lucky, or professional a counterterrorist force might be, there were bound to be casualties among the hostages.

What exactly were "acceptable" losses? Nobody had bothered to give Saxon any hard numbers.

For good reason: the politicians weren't about to put a price tag on human life. That little detail had been left, as usual, to the discretion of the shooters in theater. Saxon also knew that many politicians, and even some senior Pentagon staff, believed that if it said so in the field manuals and military textbooks, then it had to go down that way in the real world.

As commander in the field, Saxon was the soldier on point. He'd either reap the glory or suffer the blame. The politicos would win either way, no matter how it went down. If too many innocents bought it, the pols would legislate some more bills and spend some more bucks.

Yeah, they'd make some speeches, too—that was a given. If things got too sticky, Saxon could even face a court-martial—Abu Ghraib in 2005 and Ching Mao in 2009 made it clear that just because you followed orders didn't mean you couldn't do time in a federal stockade.

But no use griping about it, Saxon thought. He'd gotten his orders and now he had to execute them.

Same bullshit, different mission. As usual, nothing mattered to the brass and politicians besides getting the damn job done, and taking the credit once the grunts had cleared the war zone.

7.

SEA BASE ALPHA

SAXON CLEARED SECURITY AND RODE THE ELEVATOR
down into the *George Kennan*'s hold, where he was
greeted by a contingent of his executive officers.
Sergeants Berlin Hirsch and Mainline saluted Saxon as
the elevator doors opened and Saxon stepped into the
artificial glare of the ship's vast floodlighted interior.

Both Marines wore battle dress in the form of
NATO woodland cammies—trousers bloused over
spit-shined combat boots—and black berets emblazoned with the ball, anchor, and globe emblem of the
U.S. Marine Corps, but with the addition of a large,
crimson number one prominent in the foreground,
flanked by a grinning skull on the right and a spitting

sea cobra on the left. Shoulder patches bearing the same emblem identified the wearers as members of an elite combat formation that was arguably the toughest fighting unit on the face of the earth: Marine Force One.

Each of the two G-3s wore holstered sidearms, in Hirsch's case a Glock P-229 in military hip harness, while Mainline carried a Sig 9-millimeter semiautomatic in a fast-draw shoulder rig.

Personal weapons were largely a matter of personal choice among the members of the elite unit. Since all Force One personnel had to be checked out on every major small-arms weapon in the world, giving the troops wide latitude in this area helped keep the entire unit up to speed on assault weaponry of all types. The sole exception to the rule was MF-1's standard use of the bullpup Krinkov AKR assault rifle instead of the standard U.S.-issue M-16 or M-4 rifles. The force was unanimous in finding the AKR superior in the field in firepower, controllability, and ease of maintenance.

Saxon, having made the trip from Lejeune where his A-uniform days as staff at the Pentagon were a rapidly fading memory, was attired similarly to the Marines who greeted him in the hold of the *Kennan*. Unlike Hirsch and Mainline, though, he wasn't packing a sidearm, and he also had stripes instead of chevrons on his black beret and shoulder patch.

Saxon had earned his commissions the hard way, by the numbers, but he was yet to fully accept that he was now a full bird colonel and might one day even rise to the rank of general. In his mind he remained the young Marine lieutenant who had gotten his first taste of combat in Iraq more than two decades before. That seemed to him to have been a far longer time ago than it actually was, but the numbers didn't lie.

Between then and now had come the resurgence of the Soviet Union, the birth of the global terrorist Nexus from the ashes of bin Laden's al-Qaida organization, and the global terror spree known as Strike Day, which had dwarfed the devastation of 9/11 by several orders of magnitude.

Since the dawn of the twenty-first century, filled in hindsight with the promise of global peace, the world seemed to have slid down into the mouth of hell since September 11, 2001, with the false peace eroding into a permanent state of global emergency. War, terror, flood, famine, disasters natural and man-made, all continued to plague humankind as the twenty-first century went into its third decade.

Among other things, this chronic state of emergency had brought Marine Force One into existence as a fire hose to be turned on when needed to douse the flames of new conflict before they spread into a wildfire of death and destruction.

"Welcome aboard, boss," Hirsch told his commanding officer. "We've been working our asses off getting set up here, but we're almost done."

"We're ready for an inspection tour, boss," Mainline put in. "If you are."

"Sure, show me whatcha got," Saxon answered.

"We got plenty, boss."

The three combat veterans proceeded toward the forward sections of the hold, passing through several security checkpoints manned by MPs toting submachines with high-capacity clips in the mag wells. At each checkpoint Saxon's two horse handlers gave him the nickel tour of what the sector held.

First, Saxon inspected the mobile wheeled and tracked armor. Its ranks were made up of several different types and configurations of combat vehicles, all intended to support a wide range of combined arms operations.

Most of the combat vehicles sat on the deck plates arranged in neat lines. A lot of the gear was still being fitted out for operations, though, and was being worked on by an assortment of mechanics, weapons and electronics technicians, spot welders, and painters.

The various types of vehicles had rolled onto the *Kennan* at dockside but needed to be checked out, maintained, and in many cases even refitted while the RORO ship was under way.

In maintenance sections on the outskirts of the parking area some of these military vehicles were getting their original factory paint jobs chemically stripped to the bare steel, while others, already having gone through the process, were receiving new camouflage paint jobs that reflected woodland or desert operating environments.

Marine weapons technicians were also busily at work, removing or adding heavy machine-gun mounts, TOW launcher emplacements, and other special combat refittings. Force One's operations spanned the globe, and its gear reflected the spec ops unit's earth-girdling mission.

Vehicles were constantly being driven into and out of the parking areas as Force One's high-mobility equipment was being checked out and modified, while utility vehicles of various types, from workhorse high-lows to fast, electric-powered two-man scooters whipped past the three men in combat fatigues on their way to any of the dozens of jobs going on simultaneously throughout the vast hold.

The mingled scents of acrid spray paint, of ozone

sparked from the air by welding torches, of pungent diesel exhaust and gasoline fumes, all combined into a familiar odor that was pleasant to Saxon's nostrils, an odor that reminded him of the action of warfare. He smiled, comparing the atmosphere here to the sterile, air-conditioned ambience he'd breathed for the past six months while chained to a desk at the Puzzle Palace.

Once again, since General Patient K. had officially handed him his new orders, Saxon felt like a just-released prisoner. It was good to be back in harness. For him it was really being back in the world.

Saxon spoke encouragingly to some of the Marines working on the war-fighting vehicles, and then he and his two execs climbed into a free scooter, with Hirsch behind the wheel, Saxon in the passenger seat, and Mainline sitting a little uncomfortably on the scooter's sloping rear end. The ride didn't take long, but it gave Hirsch a chance to quickly take Saxon around the spacious hold of the cavernous cargo vessel and show him around a little bit more.

The trio soon arrived at the MF-1 Sea Base Alpha operations command center, which was at the extreme end of the hold. Here they were waved through the final security checkpoint. Once having cleared it, they jumped off the scooter and were confronted by a

----

metal stairway that rose better than a story above the level of the deck.

The MF-1 ops center was bilevel, with a large, square platform of welded steel plate raised twenty-five feet off the main deck level by steel I-beam supports. Below, between the square described by the four I-beams, was the ops center's lower section, with a higher ratio of soundproof-screened conference areas to data terminals and lacking the array of wide, flat-panel video screens that loomed over opposite ends of the upper portion of the ops center.

The screens—Doc Jeckyll, who ran the show, referred to them as his "god screens"—were set up on black-painted steel struts, and their effect was very much the same as the screens found at large sports arenas. They were linked via LAN connections to the ten data terminals that had been installed in modular workstations that dominated the upper portion of the MF-1 ops center and formed about a third of the total work area of the lower level.

With Mainline and Hirsch leading the way, Saxon climbed the metal stairs better than a score of feet to the upper level, where Doc Jeckyll awaited his CO's arrival. The Doc had a big smile on his lean, Nebraska farm boy's face that showed how eager he was to show off his gaggle of new toys. Jeckyll had a lot of them and had been having a lot of fun playing with them in recent days, just like he'd done as a boy growing up on a dairy farm in the Midwest.

The main difference was that it was a hell of a lot more fun right now, and nobody ever had to milk a computer first thing in the morning.

8.

TACTICAL SURPRISE

AL-SHARQ ALWAYS HAD KNOWN THAT THE PERFIDIOUS Russians would turn against him in the end. He was a Bedouin, and he'd grown up listening to stories of treachery for gain in the remorseless existence of the desert nomads from the wise lips of his grizzled elders.

The Libyan dictator reflected on those bygone days. He recalled the black tents pitched in the dazzling whiteness of the sands, the constant presence of the baking desert sun, and the seemingly endless expanse of desert that stretched away to distant hills near the coast. He also remembered the constant movement from place to place of his tribe, for the nomadic

Bedouins never remained in one place for very long, never set down roots, never attached themselves to any one spot of land. Instead they migrated with the seasons, their movements, like those of the desert beasts, determined by the availability of the necessities of life in the harsh lands they occupied—the presence of water and food—and, of equal importance, the absence of enemies.

In hindsight, it was the enemies of his kinsmen that had kindled the fire in his heart that had driven him remorselessly toward the heights of power, for had it not been for those enemies, Mohammed al-Sharq might never have reached the pinnacle of leadership.

As a child al-Sharq had known of Tripoli as almost a city in a dream. Its whitewashed houses, its domed and cunningly fluted minarets rising on magnificent towers high above the crowded, teeming alleys, its many bazaars rife with all manner of exotic wares, most of all, the powerful men who ruled all of Libya from its beautiful palaces—all of this seemed unreal to a child reared in the vast emptiness of the Cyrenaican desert.

And yet, one day, the Shark's tribal enemies, in league with the Americans and Europeans who had established their hated presence on Libyan soil following their evil crusader wars, and who had even turned the

- -

once noble Qaddafi into a vile puppet who sniveled and cowered at their every threat—these tribal enemies moved against al-Sharq's people in an attempt to wipe them off the face of the earth.

The attack came in the dead of night, when the Bedouins were asleep. Al-Sharq's images of the assault were confused. He recalled only the cries of fear, the reports of automatic fire, the bursting of mortar shells, the sudden flashes made by explosions and flame, the shouts of his kinsmen being slaughtered, and later the even more terrible silence that fell upon the still, dark land in the killings' aftermath.

How his mother had managed to hide them both he did not know, but she had found some crevice in the landscape into which to crawl, and there they hid from the violence and the terror around and above them. Later, his mother placed al-Sharq in the care of relatives who lived in a town. Al-Sharq had never seen a town before. Stranger still, his kinsmen were members of the Libyan military, and when he reached the age of young manhood, it was decided that it was in Qaddafi's Army of the People's Revolution that the fledgling soldier would find a career and a permanent place in society.

In only a few years the young soldier had distinguished himself by his abilities as a warrior. His

----

promotion to full colonel was so swift as to anger many of his peers who had been passed over for promotion. This didn't count for much, for with al-Sharq's promotion came a new posting to Tripoli, where these same abilities soon gained him entrance into the inner circles of Qaddafi's senior military staff.

At first al-Sharq had been awed by both the presence of Libya's legendary ruler and by actually living in Tripoli, the city of his boyhood dreams. Before long, however, al-Sharq's high spirits began to be dampened by the corruption he saw all around him. He was especially incensed by the weakness Libya's leaders showed when confronted by the Americans. They seemed to grovel like desert dogs before these foreigners.

In time he learned something that disturbed him even more. It had been Qaddafi who had sanctioned American-trained covert action teams that had moved clandestinely across the interior desert regions on search-and-destroy missions against suspected al-Qaida terrorists. In reality the Americans had been duped by the Bedouin tribesmen with whom they were allied into staging attacks on the encampments of the Bedouins' enemies. It was such an attack that had destroyed al-Sharq's village and slaughtered his family.

From that moment the Shark became obsessed by a sense of destiny. At last he knew why he had come so far, from the desert wastes of Cyrenaica to the gleaming mansions of Tripoli—it was his place to topple the tyrant Qaddafi and take over the reins of power. Learning that there were others in the Libyan military who felt the same, al-Sharq waited and planned. When the moment came, Qaddafi's fate was sealed. The Americans' groveling dog was silenced by a bullet from al-Sharq's own pistol, and his family honor was finally avenged.

The Shark's thoughts jumped back to the present.

Yes, there had been no other course to follow. It had been inevitable that once the Americans and Europeans had been thrown out of Libya for good he would align himself and his nation with the neo-Soviet Union. The NSU was not only the closest major regional power next to Egypt or Iran—both of which it dwarfed in every regard—but it also was a resurgent superpower whose aim, like his own, was to challenge the hated Americans and their Western economic trading partners and military allies everywhere in the world.

In return for having received military aid from the Russians, the Libyan dictator had been prepared to make a number of strategic concessions, and he'd made them gladly after the promised modern weaponry and technical staff had arrived in Tripoli. This much was to have been expected.

HIS THOUGHTS DRIFTED BACK TO THOSE HEADY DAYS when he'd first made his pact with the Russian Bear. He had just moved into the presidential palace in Tripoli vacated by his defunct predecessor and was full of the heady wine of success. The palace coup and social revolution that followed in its wake had taken him to heights of power he'd never dreamed he'd ever reach, and media coverage of the Americans and Europeans staging a hasty mass exodus from the shores of Tripoli had caused the hearts of his countrymen to brim over with pride.

The Russians were eager to assist him in every way, practically falling over themselves to give him money, weapons, even provide agricultural assistance and help to set up vast industrial parks capable of producing consumer goods on a scale that could compete with anyone, including the Koreans and the Chinese.

Now, though, the Soviets were planning to go entirely too far. It was obvious that the Russians were on the verge of attempting to do here in Libya what they tried in Afghanistan near the end of the Cold War era.

Tripoli wasn't Kabul, however, nor was the father colonel some weakling of a ruler who spent more time on Swiss vacations than he did attending to affairs of state.

The Libyan Shark might have been any number of things, but one thing he wasn't was weak and another was *absent*. Tripoli was the center of al-Sharq's power, and he left it only with reluctance, under heavy guard and for as brief a time as possible.

The Shark was a natural-born predator. Like his namesake, he could scent the blood odor of trouble from a long way off. Also like a shark, the Libyan dictator swam even while he slept. He was remorseless in building his bastions and jealous of every iota of the power he commanded.

If the Russians thought that they could turn Tripoli into another Kabul they were sadly mistaken. Instead, al-Sharq would kick them out, like al-Sadat had done in Egypt.

The Shark was cunning. He'd expected a move

like the one the Russians were now trying to pull on him, and he'd devised a plan to deal with it.

IT WAS TIME TO PUT IT INTO OPERATION.

"Comrades," the Shark said to those assembled around the gleaming polished boardroom table in the meeting room adjacent to his spacious office in his presidential palace.

"The enemy of my enemy is my friend. This saying all of you know. It is an ancient one."

There was murmured assent and nodding of heads. One or two of the military and political leaders assembled in the conclave mouthed a subdued *inshallah*.

"Yet we equally know that there are those enemies with whom normally no accommodation can be made. Such enemies are as the desert jackals and the scorpions and snakes of the hot sands. They are unworthy of friendship."

Again the Libyan Shark's advisers, underlings, and yes-men nodded and sent up praise to Heaven. Most wondered what he was leading toward. The Shark smiled at them and paused.

He had hoped none of them noticed his use of the word "normally." He was about to use it again.

"Normal," he said. "Ah, what a word, gentlemen. It is a sweet word, is it not?"

The Shark paused only a second, and went on, "But these are not normal times. As we speak, my esteemed comrades in *jamahiriya*, as we convene here, my worthy generals, our nation is threatened by the invasion of the Russian imperialists. Their Antonovs carry troops and enough gear to equip a division. They are planning to take us over. Do you want this?"

His last words were nearly shouted.

"*No!* Death to the invaders!"

It was, noted the father colonel, his sycophantic minister of state, Saidal Fagih. As usual, Fagih was one step ahead of the rest of the pack, almost bursting out of his skin with eagerness to be the first to shout pleasing words to his leader.

There was applause at this, especially when the father colonel joined in the clapping with gusto, and then others began to rise and try to outdo Fagih's outburst of patriotic zeal. Before very long the council chamber rang with shouts and curses, wild oaths of allegiance to the Libyan Motherland, emotional pledges to spill the Crusaders' canine blood, and similar epithets, proclamations, and boasts.

Al-Sharq listened patiently, a faint smile playing across his thin lips. He listened as the crescendo boiled over into chaos as his advisers became so worked up they almost came to blows in their excitement.

Then, without warning, the Shark drew his pistol and pulled the trigger.

The shot fired at the ceiling went clean through the roof. The Shark of Tripoli suspected it might—he'd used his gold-plated .44-caliber Smith & Wesson.

The sudden crack of a bullet rapidly exiting the barrel of the .44 was loud enough to stop traffic on a busy street. In the confines of the room it sounded louder than Ragnarok.

The sound, the cloud of acrid cordite smoke drifting across the meeting table, and the sight of al-Sharq holding the gun in his hand brought the commotion to an immediate standstill—and sent everybody diving for cover.

Recovering their wits and their dignity, the Shark's councillors also began to regain their feet. Sheepishly and—to their leader's relief, silently—they one by one climbed back into their chairs.

The Shark found it pleasant to look around him at the dumbfounded expressions, tousled hair, and open mouths of Libya's most feared and respected commanders.

How the people would enjoy such a sight! But they'd never see it. Like the private viewing of the luscious asses of his many mistresses, the Shark coveted certain things for his private pleasure alone.

"Comrades," he began again, holstering the .44.

"We thank you for your willingness to die for our nation. Yet this is not possible. You are all needed. Alive and well. To lead us into future glory, not to bow and scrape before the Russian hordes, these barbarians at the gates of Libya."

The others were silent. That was good.

"You are thinking this: What can we do? We have not the ability to fight these Cossacks who would trample us beneath their horses' hooves. You are thinking, perhaps the European Defense Force, possibly?"

The leader grinned and paused again.

"Fagih, tell them."

Saidal Fagih stood up.

"Our esteemed leader has already asked the EDF for assistance. They have deliberated but have so far done nothing."

"Nor will they," said al-Sharq, gesturing for Fagih to be seated. Good puppet that he was, Fagih sank back down as though tugged by invisible strings.

"So who will be our allies in this contest with a giant power? Who will we call upon to aid us in our hour of great challenge. Perhaps the Americans?"

Al-Sharq didn't even need Fagih to answer this

question. Not when the U.S. Sixth Fleet was prowling around the Med. The Shark knew through his very good intelligence sources that the Americans were as concerned as he was, but might well stop short of armed conflict with the Russian Bear.

As it was, the Americans' diplomatic efforts were behind the sudden holding pattern to which the Soviet aircraft had switched. Finally, should the Americans stop the Russians, they themselves would take over, and there was no stopping the United States once its leaders made up their minds to act.

"No, not the Americans either. Then who?" he asked rhetorically. "*Who* shall it be?"

The Shark saw by the looks on the faces of his councillors that none of them had an answer. That didn't surprise him.

"Well, my esteemed comrades, you will all soon know the answer to this question. But first you will all take an oath of silence, punishable by death if broken, to keep secret that which you are about to behold in this room."

An aide passed around pens and legal forms. The papers restated what the father colonel had just said. A word of any of what was about to be revealed would result in summary execution. The forms were collected, and the aide withdrew. Some noticed that al-Sharq

---

nodded at the young soldier in presidential palace dress whites.

"And now, my comrades, you will see the ancient proverb made manifest, and you shall understand its import."

THE DOOR OPENED AGAIN AND QUICKLY CLOSED. There was the sound of combat boots rapping against the polished terra-cotta floor of the spacious office, but it was drowned out by the loud murmur of surprised expressions that burst from the lips of the Libyan advisers.

To the Shark it appeared like the effect was greater in some ways than when he'd drawn his gun.

Indeed, he half expected to see some of them duck under the table. The Libyan strongman also knew that while his generals were dumbstruck by the sight of the man who'd just entered the room, they were too afraid to speak.

They had, after all, just seen the devil himself stride into their midst, the mortal enemy that was, in their minds, worse than Satan himself.

Standing before them, as big as life in olive drab paratrooper fatigues, his beret angled against his head, was the Black Dove.

General Dove ben Ami.

The most hated soldier in the Israeli Defense Force was now *here*, right in this room.

Stranger still, their leader rose to walk toward him, and his hand did not hold a gun but was extended in greeting.

9.

SEARCH AND DESTROY

THE PLAN HAD BEEN ON TIM "SKULL" JONES'S MENTAL back burner since all the "troublemakers" on the cruise had been rounded up in the first hours of the terrorist takeover and tossed in the brig. The tangos—that's what they'd called them back in Skull's old days with Naval intelligence—had thrown Jones and a number of others in the lockup. The roundup had snared all the Banshees aboard, but the seajackers also netted other guys, all of whom had some present or past connection to law enforcement or skills that might pose a threat to the tangos. It had happened so fast that there was no way the tangos couldn't have planned for it to go down that way.

The speed and efficiency of the roundup also meant that the terrorists must have checked out the cruise liner's passenger manifest in advance of their takeover and had drawn up a list of potential problem passengers. They probably had other lists, too. Hostage lists, for example. Maybe even lists showing who was expendable and could be whacked and who might prove valuable in negotiations.

This not only showed meticulous planning by the terrorists, it also attested that they had managed to carry out a deep penetration of the cruise line's most secure computer databases. From the complexity of the assault and takeover the assumption that the tangos even had pipelines into government and private computer networks wasn't that much of a stretch either.

These fuckers had checked everything out from top to bottom, and if they'd prepared as carefully for this one contingency, and drawn up lists, they'd probably made as careful preparations for every other phase of the hijacking at sea.

They seemed to have good equipment, too. The guards were armed with bullpup automatic rifles and submachine guns, and they all wore nearly identical black uniforms. The bullpen cages in which Jones and the other "problem cases" were held prisoner had obviously been part of the highjackers' preparations and had been set up right away—not all were ready for occupancy when the first batch of captives were taken into the hold. The cages had either been specially hauled aboard or had somehow been stowed away as cargo prior to the *KA III*'s departure from Aruba.

This, of course, all translated to the terrorists being unstoppable because they held all the aces. How did you defeat an opponent as powerful as that? Jones was a poker player, and he knew that if you were dealt a losing hand you had but one option if you aimed to win: *bluff*.

Controlled chaos. That was going to be the way Jones and his group of problem cases were going to make a lot of other problems for the tangos. Most of the guys in the bullpens would wind up staying where they were, behind the chain-link fences, for the duration. To accomplish the objective, a guy had to be ready to make the ultimate sacrifice; a dude had to be ready to die. If you were ready for the big sky-out, then you could use chaos as a net to catch and immobilize your enemy. Then, if you were lucky, you could defeat and destroy him.

Jones and a couple of his brigmates had that gung-ho dedication; the rest of the prisoners didn't. At least there were enough recruits for his suicide squad so that he didn't have to draw lots or similar bullshit.

Jones had tried to get more people involved with his plan. He had one argument to recruit them, but it was the most persuasive argument in the world.

They were all going to die anyway.

It was as clear as day to Jones that the terrorists were on a martyrdom mission. They were going to die, and they were going to go out taking as many nontangos with them to wherever the fuck it was that terrorists went when they cashed in their chips. He'd picked up all the signs just by watching and attempting to communicate with the guards. They were all itching to die for Allah or some bullshit like that. There was no doubt in Skull's mind.

Communication with the enemy. That was the first stage of the plan.

Phase two: escape.

Phase three: shit, that was too advanced for Skull's tired brain right that moment. Phases one and two were fuckin' hard enough.

At least the plan for phase one was pretty simple: the Banshees had to get past the guards. This was easier said than done, though. The guards were rotated regularly in what was obvious to Jones was an effort to prevent a rapport with the prisoners that might lead to a relaxation of vigilance from developing.

No rapport with the guards was desired by the terrorists, and they'd planned for this, too.

But Jones had one secret weapon.

Monk Meadows's wife's hot little ass.

Before boarding the cruise liner in Aruba, Jones had spent a couple of weeks soaking up the sun, lying on the white sand beach, gambling, and drinking.

Jones's commercial real-estate business in New Mexico was doing very well, and the day trades he did on the side had made him a small fortune in penny stocks. Sure, sometimes he wanted to laugh at his clients for letting themselves get ripped off by grossly overpriced property buys, and he knew the commodities that he was trading were junk securities that further fucked up the American economy, but if he didn't make a wad of dough, somebody else would. So fuck it—it might as well be him.

Anyway, what he did for a living wasn't illegal—what those terrorist scuts did, that was a crime. And Monk's wife's ass was going to act as a kind of Trojan horse to open the gates of Troy on this here mission. Jones found it hard to keep a straight face as he looked over at Monk, who sat in a corner at the other end of the steel mesh monkey cage.

Yeah, he'd enjoyed showing off the missus in

Aruba. And she was certainly something to look at—
an eight face on a ten body.

And horny as hell. Monk didn't mind one bit. He
enjoyed letting her do her thing. Sometimes he even
liked to watch. Jones had taken full advantage of
Monk's generosity. Now Stella was about to do her
thing for the sacred cause of freedom.

Using tap codes, they'd managed to get the word
out and up to the liner's main levels that Stella was to
be nice to certain visitors. She was the payoff for two
of the terrorist guards who got their jollies in return
for lenience and special favors to the prisoners.

These two terrorists were both from some fucked-
up snake pit in the mountains of Yemen or some chick-
enshit shantytown in Outer Mongolia, Jones couldn't
remember which. They looked like Mongolians—sort
of, anyway. But they were no Mongolian idiots when it
came to appreciating some fine trim like what Stella
had on her.

Once those boys got themselves a taste of that
blond dynamite that was waiting for them in stateroom 507, they went bananas. They'd probably been
used to humping dromedaries and she-goats, or women
who looked and smelled like dromedaries and she-
goats, and now . . . *this*.

It messed their minds. It was like 9/11 for their

dicks. And they were only too eager to do some favors in return for more of that fine U.S. Grade A poontang.

Jones was playing one of them . . . he thought of him as the weak link, though he didn't know his name. He'd been trying to get the tango to open the cell and let him out a little—just a tiny taste of freedom—and then back into the monkey cage. And Weak Link had finally given in and promised him that tonight, at 4:00 A.M., when he was back on duty and the ship was quiet, he'd give him ten minutes.

No more.

There was a consideration to be met, of course. Stella would have to do something special with Weak Link later on in payment.

Jones had to use every ounce of strength to keep from strangling the fucker as Weak Link described, in almost unintelligible broken English, what he intended to do with Stella when treat time rolled around. Jones didn't know what it was exactly, but it was somehow connected with Weak Link putting something made of silver, or of silvery metal, on the end of his pecker. Skull thought he wanted to fuck Stella in the ass, but he wasn't sure and frankly didn't much care.

Whatever his fantasy might have been, Weak Link smiled like the Cheshire cat when he'd told Skull about it.

Well, he'd never get his chance. Unknown to Weak Link the other guard, Dog Breath, had let them have two plastic hair combs, which, of course, had painstakingly been sharpened down to deadly spikes.

Jones remembered how, as a kid spending the summers at a beachside bungalow, he'd made daggers out of Good Humor Popsicle sticks that were effective enough to stab kids who gave him problems and send them to the big white hospital a few blocks away. These prison daggers would work even better.

Well, it was almost time to roll. Jones gave Monk the high sign, telling him to get his shit together for the breakout. Though they weren't allowed watches or other timepieces, they could figure the time to within a few minutes of accuracy. Jones figured it was now a little before one in the morning.

Soon . . . the break would come real fucking soon. Jones turned away from Monk, wondering about how the final story of the mission would play once it was all over and the terrorists were dead. How would the media describe Stella's role in all this?

Probably the same way as the Bible did, Skull figured. Nowhere does it say, "Judith balled the Philistine king Holofernes to the point of total physical exhaustion. While Holofernes, fucked mindless, lay there trying to get his mojo working again, Judith got up, pretending she needed to take a piss, and then bashed his head in with a handy wine goblet."

Nope. Not a word of that shit in the Bible. That's for sure. Jones could just picture the president addressing the nation. He's painting the whole affair in patriotic colors. Talks about the brave American heroes who saved the lives of hundreds of innocent hostages onboard. Soon he gets to Stella's role in the drama.

"And their secret weapon, the bravest warrior in the entire group, my fellow Americans, was a wife and homemaker, by the name of Stella. By baking tasty fudge brownies in a homemade oven she cleverly manufactured from soup cans and Sterno, Stella enticed these godless foreigners who'd never tasted good ol' down-home American cooking from the path of evil to the side of righteousness."

Or maybe the prez would even get a little closer to the truth, quoting from the Bible and concluding, "You see—and I checked this out with the chief historian at the Smithsonian Institution personally about this—Viagra hadn't been invented yet in those days, so the Philistine king couldn't keep it up all night, like I can with the first lady. Well, Stella did pretty much the same to the hijackers that Judith did to them godless, evil Philistines."

Yeah. That's how the asshole politicians would spin it. Stella's horny ass would become hot fudge brownies wrapped in Old Glory or a modern version of a Bible story.

Fucking lies and bullshit, the old mushroom treatment, that's what the pols excelled at. Especially this jerk of a president. Hell. Jones thought; Bush, Clinton, Bush again, and then the *other* Clinton were bad enough. This guy Claymore, forget it.

Well, it didn't matter what they ultimately called Stella's role in this escapade. Only two things really counted.

First, rescuing the ship and being the hero of the hour. Second, making sure that Tim "Skull" Jones got the credit he richly deserved for being the only guy with balls, brains, and a plan on the whole damn motherfuckin' ship.

Zero hour was fast approaching.

Jones signaled to Monk to have the others get ready. They all knew their parts by now. Just like Stella did.

SKULL JONES MIGHT NOT HAVE BEEN AS SANGUINE about the course of future events had he listened to a speech the leader of the hijackers gave a little later. It was a speech that showed that the Evangelist had strategies similar to Skull's own.

"Controlled chaos. Modulated discord. The injection of white noise into a symphonic masterpiece."

Carlos Evangelista paused and looked around at the men and women seated around the swimming pool in the *KA III*'s spacious Nautical Lounge. The waters of the swimming pool were calm, but every so often something caused a wave to mar the level surface. Evangelista brought the microphone to his lips again and went on.

"Coherent insanity. Placid turmoil. Opposites reconciled in a neutron particle accelerator."

He stopped and smiled at his audience.

"This," he concluded, "is *la revolución*. It is its essence, its motivating factor, its reason for being. For only in revolution can those forces in the world that are direct opposites be reconciled and made whole in an entirely new synthesis."

That's why he had brought his inner cadre of terrorists to the poolside. He must teach them of revolution. He must make them understand. He said he would show them in a way with which mere words could never compare.

The Evangelist snapped his fingers. Those watching him saw a look of enraptured expectation play

----

across his triangular face and flash from the glittering studs between his slitted eyelids. All the head lacked was a pair of horns, thought one onlooker.

It was that kind of face, and in the reflection of the spotlighted waters of the pool there was also a dull red sheen playing across it to complete the resemblance to the devil himself.

Above the Evangelist, hidden somehow in the shadows of the ceiling, a chain descended. Two figures dangled from it. Both were stark naked. Both looked American. Fat bellies, faces out of a Rockwell print. Mostly, though, it was the crude Stars and Stripes that had been painted on their bellies on the Evangelist's orders that was the giveaway.

The chains continued to descend and the two passengers went down with them until the soles of their feet just touched the water in the pool.

After that, the previously calm surface began to churn furiously. It soon became a frothing white wake that was quickly stained a malignant dark red as the legs, then the torsos of the victims, disappeared beneath the surface.

Evangelista ordered the crane to pull the chains up. The torsos had been sheared in half, as if by a buzz saw.

"Piranha."

His explanation was a single, eloquent word.

"Brought from my native country. Carnivores of the Amazon. You have seen nothing until you've seen such fish strip a live cow down to a skeleton in five minutes flat."

Another gesture and the bodies were lowered again, this time until the waters completely covered the corpses' heads. When the chains were again raised only tatters of flesh remained on the heavy steel hooks that had skewered the bodies of the passengers.

"Controlled chaos. Intelligent stupidity. Monochromatic color. Dynamic torpidity. Think well of this display, *mis compañeros*," the Evangelist said before turning to leave.

"You will need to learn the lesson I have just imparted before this enterprise is over. Should you fail to learn it, you will, I am afraid, pay for your ignorance with your lives. *¡Viva la revolución!*"

THE SOUND OF THE CHILL WATER RUSHING BENEATH the hull had begun to frighten him. Sometimes it seemed to become a chorus of voices, urging him to do things he didn't want to do, urging him to go out and take revenge on the hijackers.

He told himself that it was hunger and thirst that

made him hear the voices—that he was hallucinating. It changed nothing. The waters spoke to him. They were ashamed of and angry with him. They called him a coward. If you were a man, they said, you would kill at least some of them. Even one would be revenge enough. Revenge for what they did to your wife and children when they came aboard, and took you from among the living.

Yet he continued to do nothing, continued to find sanctuary in the cold and the darkness where the sea was only three inches from his body and the vibrations of the keel played across the spine of his back like the caressing hand of the Reaper fondling his next dupe, like a tree farmer fondling a peach ripening on a low-hanging branch.

He didn't care. He was numb with remorse. He stayed where he was, listening to the rush of the water and the knowledge that only a mere three inches of steel separated the rest of the ship from millions of cubic feet of ice-cold ocean that would rush through any hole and quickly swamp the ship until it sank to the bottom.

And now the voices in the sea were telling him something else. At last they were telling them who they really were. They were the dead. The spirits of all who'd been lost at sea and now lived in the deeps of Davy Jones's locker.

He listened to them babble, not caring what they kept telling him to do . . . until one pair of voices piped up above the rest, and suddenly made him sit up, his entire body trembling.

"Find explosives. Set them off right here, where you've lain for so long. Erase your cowardice."

"No!"

For the first time he cried out in the darkness of the deepest part of the ship's vast hold, not caring if anyone heard his shouts.

There was no mistaking the voices he now heard. They belonged to the ghosts of those killed in the hijacking who roamed the ship as vagrant spirits.

"Find explosives," they went on. "Send her to the bottom."

He clapped the palms of his hands to the bowls of his ears and screamed in the hellish night of his cold, steel tomb.

10.

A TURN FOR THE WORSE

THE BLACK DOVE'S APPEARANCE IN THE COUNCIL chamber of the father colonel's presidential palace in Tripoli came as an electrifying shock to the Libyan deputies of the People's Revolution. The dictator's uniformed and medal-bedecked yes-men would have been twice as bowled over if they'd known that at that very moment three Israeli stealth warplanes were preparing to launch from concealed runways hidden amid arid mountains and remote deserts in the Middle East.

The VSTOL Scorpion jets were indigenously manufactured Israeli air superiority fighters. The mission of the Scorpions was twofold. They would act as forward observation scout planes, their radars scanning

----

the skies for the Russian Antonov transports that had launched from Soviet airspace two days previous.

They would also fly CAP—combat air patrol—to defend the second Israeli air asset in the skies against the threat of enemy attack from Russian "frontal" or tactical air, especially from fast and stealthy MiG MRF fighters.

This other Israeli military aircraft was an AWACS aircraft, also indigenously produced, called the Phalcon because of its hawklike nose section that loomed above a large sensor bulge directly beneath the cockpit. The Phalcon's far more powerful search-and-track radar and electronic warfare systems constituted the second of a three-tiered layer that the Israelis had put in place for the mission.

The third layer was an orbital platform codenamed Tel Aviv. This was the key weapon platform that the Israelis had deployed in the theater or, more accurately, high above the theater. Tel Aviv was similar to the U.S. military's Cerberus N-EMP satellite, whose existence itself was a closely guarded secret. Cerberus could be closely likened to an enormous Duracell orbiting ten miles up, beyond the edge of the exosphere, the farthest edge of atmospheric space.

Cerberus, a flattened steel toroid half the size of a football stadium and containing a small nuclear power plant that charged the banks of power cells making up the bulk of its mass, could direct a high-energy particle beam down through the earth's atmosphere to strike high-value targets on the planet's surface. Cerberus was an option of last resort, and the mantle of secrecy that cloaked it was one of the things that made it effective.

Unseen, unknown, striking invisibly from afar, the particle beam weapon had been responsible for numerous incidents both in military engagements and in peacetime "accidents" that had long been the subject of international debate and the source of much conspiracy theory.

A few years earlier, Cerberus had played a role in Marine Force One's mission in the mountainous cross-border regions between Turkey and Iran to halt the clandestine air transshipment of weapons, POL, and military spares to Nexus terrorist bases in Afghanistan.

Cerberus had played other roles in other engagements. Yet it remained a tightly kept military secret. Few, including the neo-Soviets, were even aware of the space weapon's existence.

But the Israelis knew about Cerberus, and had known since the Pollard affair, when the double agent in U.S. Naval Intelligence had first brought his Mossad handlers the plans for the earliest U.S. N-EMP system

----

prototypes back in the late twentieth century. Now, decades later, the Israelis had a stealthy N-EMP orbital station of their own whose cover name was Tel Aviv.

It was Tel Aviv that was to be the cornerstone of the operation against the Soviet military airlift mission to Tripoli.

The Black Dove didn't say this to his stunned listeners; he only informed them that the IDF (Israeli Defense Force) had mounted a military operation to use classified assets to turn back the Antonovs before they reached Tripoli.

"We will stop the Antonov airlift before NSU forces penetrate Libyan airspace," promised the Black Dove. "We will cut them off faster than a mohel snips a foreskin."

The Black Dove paused a moment, enjoying the confusion on the faces of his Libyan audience at the reference to circumcision. When al-Sharq laughed at the allusion, they all followed suit. After their faces had set again and they glared at him like stone gargoyles, Dove ben Ami went on.

"We are prepared to use a variety of classified military means short of open attack to gain this vital objective. Israel is taking these steps for its benefit as well as Libya's. It is in the interest of the entire Middle East to keep the Soviets out—*permanently* out."

"My honored friends," al-Sharq put in, continuing the briefing, "I have been consulting with the esteemed general for several days prior to this meeting.

"Our two nations have reached agreements beyond this episode that will prove of great mutual benefit. I will tell you also that secret talks have been taking place for some time between our respective countries."

The Shark deliberately left out that some of those secret talks, and secret treaty protocols that were connected to them, had resulted in one of the high-technology Berkut fighters lent to Libya by the Soviets to be secretly studied by Israeli military technicians to clone the technology for Israeli military use.

The Libyan dictator kept silent on this point because its revelation would have been a little too much for his cabinet members' already overwhelmed minds to handle at the moment.

In fact, anticipating that unsound minds might even begin to hatch a palace coup, the father colonel had taken certain precautions to make sure that his revelation didn't lead to revolution. The dictator's close subordinates had more bugs on their phones and computers, and in their cars, homes, and offices, than a hornet's nest had wasps.

Al-Sharq was playing for keeps, now as always.

"But back to you, General," he said to the Black Dove. "I'm sure you have much more to tell us."

The gargoyle stares turned to the Israeli, who flicked on his laser pen and aimed the red pencil beam of coherent light at the large regional map behind him.

MAJOR GENERAL BULGANIN FONDLED HIS MAKAROV sidearm and conceived bold fancies of martial magnificence and conqueror's glory—all of which naturally featured himself in the starring role.

Although his new shoulder flashes were merely days old, and although Bulganin's only experiences with combat involved field exercises and training simulations, the general had already become a second Alexander in his own mind.

Bulganin had always admired Alexander. As a child growing up in the comfortable, well-to-do Moscow neighborhood of Leninskiy Prospekt, he had thrilled to stories of the Macedonian general's glorious exploits, and these had formed the basis for his entire military life.

Now Bulganin was in seventh heaven. Today a merciful fate had at last granted him his fondest wish— to emulate the mighty Alexander.

The Antonov mission had been grounded due to

pressure from the Americans and their capitalist allies in NATO and the European Union. While veteran diplomats shuttled between Western capitals and Moscow, and the U.N. Security Council deliberated and issued proclamations and communiqués, while the gnomes of Zurich danced a jig, the Tripoli-bound airlift had been forced to land and remain grounded many miles from its planned objective.

Eventually Russia's new Stalin, Premier Timoshenko, had grown weary of playing games of state. Early that morning the Kremlin had decided that the political theater would end there and then. Timoshenko had resolved to bring the curtain crashing down on the final act of a tired comedy.

The Soviet leader had sent a bevy of diplomats to the airport and summarily put them aboard Aeroflot commercial jets back to their respective home countries. The Russian ambassador had bluntly informed the United Nations that the New Soviet Union had decided to ignore the feeble protests from other nations less bold than themselves, who feared the hardships of the warrior from which the Soviets would not finally shrink, and the grounded Antonovs had gotten new orders to take to the air as soon as they were ready and to proceed on their mission to Tripoli.

That was one order that Bulganin, as the commander of the first Antonov airlift and soon to be commander of all Soviet forces in Libya, made sure was carried out as fast as was humanly possible.

Within minutes of the order's receipt, aircrew were on their way to the waiting planes, and in under an hour's time the fleet of heavy lifters was back in action, rumbling across the starlit skies above the southern Mediterranean at forty thousand feet.

Soon the first of the big jet aircraft shuttles was in docking position for the hose-and-drogue that was dangling from one of two Ilyushin fuelbirds that was orbiting for in-flight AAR—air-to-air refueling— prior to the Antonovs' departure for Libya about a thousand miles to the south.

That had been hours ago. Bulganin had now grown bored with visiting the aircraft's flight deck and talking with the pilots, who were far more bored with him, or with vague discussions with his exec, the sullen Davidovich, about the glories of conquest and pillage that awaited the new Russian Alexander and his stalwart troops once they'd touched down on Libyan soil.

The truth was that the Soviet expedition to Tripoli was a mission in search of a plan. The Kremlin had

been hasty to act but tardy in crafting anything resembling military strategy beyond landing the planes
and offloading the troops.

Bulganin had merely been instructed to improvise,
and the Soviet leader's personal guarantee of giving
the newly minted general full assistance had been
coupled with a hearty pat on the shoulder and Premier Timoshenko's assurance of his complete faith in
the fledgling commander's expert judgment.

Not once in the many hours and days since he'd
been suddenly bidden to a meeting at the Kremlin
had it occurred to Bulganin that he was merely a
puputchick, a puppet, in the eyes of the leader: that he
was being used as a straw dog to be cast down and
burned should things go wrong and the operation take
a turn for the worse.

Nor did Bulganin suspect that his taciturn executive officer Colonel Dragun Davidovich, whom he
hardly knew, also had received orders from the Little
Stalin, as Muscovites fondly called Timoshenko, and
that these, unlike his own, held the official backing of
the GRU staff.

Bulganin would have been dismayed to learn that
those orders called for his immediate execution should
things go seriously wrong.

It would then be arranged by Colonel Davidovich

to appear as though Bulganin had gone insane and had needed to be killed to salvage the mission.

Bulganin suspected nothing of this.

Oblivious to the machinations of more cunning and more experienced men, he smoked a cigarette and fondled his pistol, fantasies of a glory he was never to attain running through his mind as the Antonovs droned on through the ebbing darkness that preceded the new and savage dawn.

11.

STRIKE VECTORS

IN GEOSTATIONARY LOW EARTH ORBIT (LEO), TEL
Aviv was being silently jockeyed into position for the
discharge of a high-energy particle beam to a target
complex many miles below.

The space station's onboard inertial navigational
system was being fed constant situational updates on
the position of the Antonov airlift from both the
Scorpion tactical fighters and the Phalcon AWACS
command and control plane, which flew beyond vi-
sual range (BVR) of the airborne echelon of Soviet
heavy lifters.

As telemetry on the targets was continually
received and updated, microprocessor-sequenced

---

chemical rocket thrusters onboard the EMP satellite fired time-coordinated bursts that nudged the orbital weapon into a precision trajectory that would maximize its lethal accuracy. While this was happening, the weapon's electrical storage cells were continuing to initialize, storing up millions of kilowatts of electrical current generated by Tel Aviv's small nuclear reactor.

It was the mission commander aboard the Israeli AWACS aircraft, a major general, who had responsibility for ordering his weapons system officer (WSO) to discharge the particle beam weapon. He would do so once he in turn informed the Black Dove by secure low-frequency radio link that Tel Aviv had acquired target lock on the Antonovs and that the orbital weapon was ready to discharge.

The mission commander had been steadily monitoring an array of computer screens on a console in a secure, screened-off section of the Phalcon's airmobile operations center.

It was clear to him that the mission was quickly entering the optimum operational window—the Antonovs were about to reach their final waypoints high above the central Mediterranean before entering Libyan airspace; the weapon's array of power cells was fully charged; the satellite weapon platform was in position and had full target acquisition of the target planes.

The mission commander now took the steps that his orders required him to take prior to triggering the space-based weapon.

He contacted the Black Dove for final instructions, informing his CO that all systems were go for firing.

In a stout command bunker beneath the walled compound of the Keriya, the headquarters of the IDF, the Israeli defense minister, Moishe Grod, waited for the Black Dove's message. Almost at the same time, an air force officer in room 2B902 of the Pentagon's NMCC, the National Military Command Center, actuated Hammer Rick, a secure satcom link to IDF headquarters in Tel Aviv. A brief exchange of code-word-level enciphered messages took place in the ensuing minutes prior to weapon discharge.

At the end of the colloquy, the operation received its final clearance to proceed.

The execution of the mission, the activation of the weapon, though Israeli, actually had U.S. backing.

A few seconds elapsed as the go codes went down the chain of command. Then, from the Keriya, came the final clearance to the mission commander.

"You are cleared for firing. Repeat. Final clearance is authorized. Good luck."

The mission commander broke squelch and informed his chief weapon system officer to initialize the orbital weapon.

And to fire when ready.

ONBOARD THE AIRBORNE TROOP CONVOY'S LEAD transport plane, Major General Bulganin had no inkling of the powerful advanced particle beam armament orbiting miles above him that was about to hurl down a bolt of lightning upon his naive and clueless head. The self-styled Alexander would soon taste the fire of the gods. He was about to be speared by the thunderbolts of Zeus. It would not be pleasant. Then again, he was no Alexander.

It took hardly a second once the space-based weapon had discharged the first EMP salvo for the supercharged electrical pulse to negotiate the dense blanket of many miles of atmosphere separating the orbiting Tel Aviv satellite and the lead Antonov, its primary target.

The first inkling that the transport plane had been hit by something unknown was the dimming of the cabin lights, followed by the aircraft's violent pitching as the Antonov's onboard navigational system temporarily locked up.

Bulganin, like the other crew personnel who shared the cabin with him, was thrown to the aircraft's hard floor as the electromagnetic pulse struck the plane full broadside. He scrambled to his feet and lurched toward the flight deck, shouldering aside his subordinates in his haste to reach the cockpit. In the flickering cabin light Bulganin heard soldiers cursing their lot as they struggled to right themselves and regain their footing.

It took Bulganin many long minutes of pushing and shoving to finally reach the flight deck, minutes that somehow seemed like years.

"What the hell happened?" he demanded of the crew dogs who controlled the plane.

"We aren't certain," replied the pilot.

"Navigation's all screwed up and, listen"—the pilot indicated the radio by a hand gesture and switched from headset comms to cabin audio—"the other planes behind us are suddenly as messed up as we are."

"How can it be?" asked Bulganin, a look of deep puzzlement crossing his regular White Russian features. "Have we been attacked?"

The flight deck crew dogs weren't puzzled at all.

"Attacked? Yes, but by an unknown weapon, comrade General," the pilot answered, and even in the dazed state that he was in, Bulganin distinctly heard the clear note of contempt in the pilot's voice. "We've been hit by something—all of the planes in the airlift have gotten hit by something. This much is clear."

"But there was no explosion, no sign of a missile—"

"Perhaps because no missile was used in the attack, comrade General."

Bulganin wasn't accepting this explanation.

"Could it have been weather? A bolt—"

Bulganin wheeled around at the sound of his executive officer's voice behind him. He turned to see Colonel Davidovich standing in the cabin doorway. A strange smile played across the colonel's mouth; an ominous smile, but the major general was too deep in shock to notice it.

Behind the colonel, Bulganin glimpsed a scene of utter panic and confusion in the flickering cabin lights. The entire plane had been hit by something invisible, yet with devastating effect.

"But how—"

"There are weapons other than missiles or artillery shells or bullets, my General. There are directed energy weapons firing particle beams. Or haven't you figured that out yet?"

Bulganin didn't like his subordinate's tone of

voice. It was devoid of respect; it dripped of inso-
lence like a snake's fangs dripped venom before it
struck, biting deep into the flesh of its poisoned
prey.

Yet before the general could utter a word in repri-
mand, Colonel Davidovich had drawn his pistol. He
pointed the gun squarely at the space between the
two top gold buttons of Bulganin's tan field tunic.

"Please remain calm," Davidovich went on with a
broad smile on his lean, angular face, sensing that his
superior officer was on the verge of doing something
terribly foolish.

This dog of a colonel possessed the face of a
Machiavelli, Bulganin again noted; a cunning, malign
face, a face with the lean and hungry look of Caesar's
executioners. A line from Shakespeare came to him
then, "Such men are dangerous."

Suddenly Bulganin began to tremble. He wished
he could wipe that self-satisfied smile off that bony,
diabolical face, but with the gun trained on him he
was utterly powerless.

Now Bulganin was afraid for his life. Worse yet,
Davidovich seemed to sense the discomfiture of his
superior officer. At the moment that the general grew
aware of his fear, the colonel inhaled deeply, as if a

new and pleasant perfume had just wafted into the air of the flight deck.

"Take this asshole's gun," the colonel said to the pilot, his voice languid, as if he were ordering champagne at a Moscow nightclub surrounded by a bevy of admiring young girls.

"What's the meaning of this?" Bulganin tried to sound in control, but his voice had a whiny, puling edge to it. His attempt to sound brave wasn't convincing.

The colonel ignored him and spoke to the pilot, keeping his pistol trained on Bulganin.

"Captain, what is the status of the aircraft? Will we have to ditch?"

"Negative, sir," the pilot answered crisply.

"As you can see if you check that scope over there, we seem to be stabilizing. The other planes are also recovering."

"How far are we as yet from Libyan airspace?"

"Still several kilometers left to transit, sir. We're close, but we have an ETA of about ten minutes yet."

"In that case you are to immediately execute a change of course and return to Moscow," the colonel instructed the pilot. "The rest of the planes, too. That is an order."

"Ignore that, Captain. That is *not* an order!"

Bulganin bellowed out the words, his voice strident.

"*I* am in command here, not this traitorous saboteur!" the general shouted at the flight deck crew.

"The colonel not only has no authority to order *anything*, but you are to place him under immediate house arrest. He does not make the rules. I do. Shoot him should he refuse to lower his gun."

The pilot and copilot looked at each other questioningly.

Neither moved a muscle.

"Oh, yes, I forgot to mention, my General," said the colonel with his insufferable dreamy air, his voice as languid as before. "You were relieved of command as of the moment I entered the flight deck."

He reached into a pocket of his tunic and pulled out a folded sheet of paper; the flash of an official GRU seal was immediately visible. He passed the orders to the pilot and copilot.

Last to see them was Bulganin. His final hopes sank then: they indeed bore the official stamp of the GRU and were signed by Rubinksy, the chief of staff.

Davidovich wasted no more words on the pitiable, doomed *paputchick*. The Soviet general secretary had appointed the colonel as Bulganin's handler. The

Kremlin leader's instructions to Davidovich were un-equivocal. Should the mission run into unforeseen problems, such as unexpected, severe attack, it was to be aborted, in which case Bulganin was to be set up as a patsy to take the brunt of the blame.

Colonel Davidovich's only remaining question concerned what sort of treasonous action to put in his debriefing report.

"Shot while trying to escape," from an old American movie, came to mind, but unfortunately that wouldn't work here. Escape to where? No, that clearly wouldn't do.

Well, he'd think of something. Davidovich had plenty of time to give his imagination free rein, and he was a man gifted with an abundant imagination.

But now, he thought, *first things first.*

Time to act.

Without further ado the colonel squeezed the pistol's trigger and sent a hypodermic flechette hurtling from the muzzle on a blast of compressed air.

The razor-tipped syringe immediately buried itself in the upper-right front of Bulganin's dress uniform.

On impact the hollow tip of the needle shot an incapacitating dose of a powerful hallucinogenic drug into Bulganin's bloodstream.

The drug acted quickly. Hardly had Bulganin become aware that he'd been shot when the air of the cabin seemed to take on strange colors and Davidovich suddenly metamorphosed into a Mephistophelian figure with horns on his head and a serpent's forked red tongue that flicked from between his lips.

"Take him to hell," he heard the red-caped figure say to demonic beings—leering djinns and capering specters—who sprang up from burning thrones to grab him by the arms and drag him down to the underworld.

And then there was darkness, and the crackling sound of eternal flames.

Colonel Davidovich bent over the figure of the general lying collapsed on the hard steel floor plates of the Antonov's flight deck. He checked for a pulse and found it.

The *paputchick* lived . . . for the time being.

Still crouched over the general's prone form, the colonel glanced up at the Antonov's pilot.

"You will be informed of what to say happened prior to this buffoon's trial for treason. Otherwise, say nothing to anyone concerning what happened here.

"Any questions?"

As expected, there were none.

"Good. Now turn this plane around and file a flight

----

plan for home. See to it the other pilots do precisely the same. That is all."

THE SHARK OF TRIPOLI READ THE DISPATCH THAT had just been handed to him. There was jubilation on his aquiline face as he looked up again and addressed the officials in the room.

"The Soviet planes are turning back. We have won, *inshallah*."

The Libyan dictator's advisers in the council chamber praised Allah for delivering them all and rushed forward to congratulate their leader on the success of his bold and unprecedented gambit.

The Israeli general who had made it possible was forgotten amid the tumult of their jubilation. The Black Dove had already slipped from the meeting room and was on his way to a waiting limousine to Uqba-bin-Nafi Airport.

General Dove ben Ami had watched the progress of the space-based weapon against the Antonov troop and matériel airlift to the Libyan capital city via a secure downlink to a laptop computer.

The laptop contained a charge sufficient to destroy it in a burst of flame should biometric sensors detect anyone but the general attempting to use it. Tel Aviv

----

had proven itself in actual combat, and the Russian attempt to establish a beachhead in the Middle East had been—at least for now—decisively crushed.

Now, with two successes to be proud of, and other matters preoccupying his mind, and a healthy desire to quit himself of Tripoli as fast as possible, the Black Dove slid into the backseat of the official staff car and told the driver to make it snappy.

He had a plane to catch.

12.

GHOST RIDERS

THE CRIES OF THE ENEMY IN PAIN—MUSIC TO THEIR ears.

The new taste of freedom—a heady, violent wine that made liquid steel flow through their limbs and made their blood take sudden wing.

The blade—crude, plastic, once a hair comb, but now sharp enough to pierce the jugular and cause fatal internal bleeding within minutes of wounding.

The crude prison weapon—a silent messenger of death. Without words its painful bite served notice on the guard they called Weak Link now that the tables were turned.

There was no need to speak. No point in anything

except swift and brutal action. Jones pushed the tip of the makeshift weapon, painstakingly honed to a needlepoint, against Weak Link's throat with one hand and shoved him backward into the cell with the other.

Strangely, Jones felt a flush of pity for his captive.

It was insane, but the guard's eyes were saucers of liquid black terror. His body had gone limp—it was almost like pushing around a helium-filled balloon. Just like that—almost as if Weak Link's body was just a thin-walled bag of hot air.

You could practically feel his helplessness, his total loss of control, as if all of the starch in him had been pissed out into a porcelain bowl. As soon as he'd felt the point of the knife against his jugular— that was it. The fucker was lost. He'd turned to slime.

Jones brushed aside the emotional upswell.

Sure, he's helpless now, Jones thought. *But five minutes ago the mother held the whip hand and he acted like Attila the Hun, didn't he? Without a gun in his hand and a mess of galvanized chain link between him and me, he's nothing.*

His mind flashed back to the minutes preceding the breakout.

Jones and the other prisoners in the five monkey cages tense, silent, expectant. Skull's lieutenants, the inner core of the "troublemakers" culled from Skull's

----

Howlin' Banshees Cycle Club inner circle, silently rehearsing the parts they were to play.

Everyone committed, spoiling for action.

Waiting for the moment to rush the guards and break for their Harleys. Trying to grab as much sleep as possible before the 4:00 A.M. zero hour, when the guard detail changed shifts and Weak Link, Dog Breath, and Mo-Mo came on duty.

Weak Link, Dog Breath, and Mo-Mo. The three terrorist stooges. Each had been given a taste of Stella's stone fine ass. Weak Link always liked to come over to Skull's cell and brag about it. He thought Stella was Jones's woman and didn't understand enough English to realize his mistake. This morning was no exception.

"I happy now," Weak Link had declaimed, sidling up to a corner of the monkey cage and leaning close. "Make good fucking. She like me, want me give more fucking tomorrow."

"Glad you enjoyed yourself," Jones had answered him. "You just stretched your dick. Now let me stretch my legs."

"Huh?"

Jones communicated by sign language that he wanted Weak Link to open the cage and let him out per their arrangement. Just like the times before, when he'd gone docilely back inside.

Each time, Weak Link's guard dropped a little lower. Each time, his suspicions became less acute. So why should now be any different?

"Yes, you walk. Okay."

Weak Link reached for the keys at his belt and gave a quick look at Dog Breath and Mo-Mo, who raised their short-barreled submachine guns to cover the cage. They weren't stupid, after all.

Jones walked outside. Cigarettes had to be provided by the guards—for security purposes, they'd insisted. Weak Link handed him a smoke and gave him a light. Weak Link smiled through the flame and his mouth worked. He was about to make another remark in pidgin English—about Stella, no doubt.

At that moment the fight broke out.

Prisoners in the next cage down the line began to shout and throw punches. Dog Breath and Mo-Mo turned and ran over. Jones moved fast, as he'd planned it. Pinning Weak Link's gun hand with the edge of his forearm, he whipped the knife end of the filed-down comb up and jabbed it into the soft underside of Weak Link's throat.

As he disarmed Weak Link, Jones risked a head turn long enough to determine that the other two guards were being swiftly overwhelmed by the prisoners who'd been throwing punches at each other a moment before but now instantly sprang at the two terrorists. Dog Breath and Mo-Mo were disarmed in the same manner as Weak Link and shoved into the prisoners' cages.

That had been mere minutes ago. Skull's heart continued to jackhammer in his chest as the adrenaline rush mounted. He had Weak Link's key ring, which unlocked a door to another room that held the keys to their bikes.

Jones led the rush to the room, threw open the door. They scrabbled to get at the keys. Then each ran to where they knew their bikes were stored.

Inside most of those bikes were the semiautomatic handguns that Skull's Howlin' Banshees had unanimously voted to stash so they could do some recreational shooting in Barbados and Marrakesh and other ports of call. Hell, they'd all been looking forward to chugging *mucho* brewskis, wineskis, and whatever other alcoholskis they could lay hands on, and shoot up the fucking desert. Now they instead were going to shoot up some badass terrorist gunslingers. Not as good, especially since they had to do it sober, but sometimes you took what you could find and liked it.

Free again, the members of Skull's Howlin' Banshees Cycle Club of Albuquerque, New Mexico, ran like fiends through the cruise ship's vast hold.

Within minutes the roar of their chopped and channeled hogs revving up and the screech of burning tire rubber as the first Banshees out of the hold popped bitchin' wheelies rang through the ship like an outlaw battle cry.

CIA DIRECTOR HAMPTON YEE HADN'T BELIEVED WHAT had now materialized on the display screen. The e-mail message on the CIA's secure Intranet had come from the deputy director of intelligence. It briefed Yee on the urgency of the fresh intel and contained a bulleted list of main talking points.

The list read:

- Secret high-level discussions among the three countries named to determine nature and scope of unilateral military action.

- Secret protocols cite determination of principals to effect regime change.

- Clandestine diversion of at least one mobile armored division as well as airborne surveillance and reconnaissance resources in the services of covert activities.

- Mobilization of key media assets of protocols' signatory nations to mold public opinion and ease transition to state of war.

- Role of United States uncertain in plans now known. So far United States appears to be excluded from direction planned by protocol signatory nations.

The DCI had carefully reviewed the raw intelligence take that accompanied the brief prepared for him by the CIA's intelligence directorate, telling his secretary to bring him a fresh carafe of piping hot black coffee. Although Yee was pressed for time with a dozen simultaneous projects, the importance of the memo was such that he devoted nearly two hours to scanning the surveillance intercepts from which the abstract had been drafted.

An old field whore who could still recall the final year or two of the Cold War, Yee fully grasped the extremely serious implications of the message, and he understood why the intelligence directorate had routed it into his CRITIC-flagged in-box.

The DCI then called a meeting of close advisers to be adjourned in half an hour's time in the secure

----

conference room adjacent to his office. He paused
for a few minutes to splash cold water on his tired,
overheated eyes and to outline the main questions
and talking points he wanted to bring up at the meeting, which, once convened, gave the CIA director
the professional consensus he felt he needed before
bringing the matter to the president.

Now, several hours after Yee had first scanned the
opening lines of the e-mail from intelligence, he was
ensconced in the backseat of a Lincoln Continental
flying the flag of the CIA director's office. The limo
had completed the twenty-minute ride along the Belt-
way from the CIA's headquarters at Langley and
crossed the Potomac over the Fourteenth Street
Bridge and gone through midmorning traffic around
the Washington Monument and Rock Ridge Park.

The director's secretary had phoned ahead, and
key documents bearing on the crisis—it was a crisis
in embryo for sure—had been transmitted by secure
Internet protocols to the White House's PROFS system, where they were being scanned by a now increasingly concerned and disturbed president.

Minutes later the DCI's limo entered the White
House grounds via the West Wing entrance gate. The
driver stopped the car long enough for his VIP passenger to climb out the back, pull his black leather

----

attaché case out after him, and stride past two smartly saluting Marine MPs, one of whom held the door to the West Wing visitors' entrance open for him in a white-gloved hand.

Once he was inside, a White House aide greeted him deferentially, taking the distinguished visitor's tan mohair coat as the DCI clipped a blue, color-coded photo ID tag to the breast pocket of his custom-tailored charcoal pinstripe suit.

"The president is waiting to see you, sir," he was told. "He's expecting you in the Oval Office."

"Thank you."

The CIA director was a frequent visitor to the White House and already knew where the president would be waiting to receive him. The DCI turned to the left and walked briskly past another cordon of Marine honor guards from the lobby into the section of the executive mansion reserved for the chief executive and cabinet-level staff only.

He wryly reflected that one did not need what James Jesus Angleton, the Central Intelligence Agency's former director of intelligence, had once labeled a "black mind" to guess where the president would be, since Travis Claymore almost always held meetings in the Oval Office, and far more infrequently the adjoining Map Room.

There were perhaps five rooms at the White House suitable for meetings with small groups, but the president was as regular as clockwork in his choices. If he had time for you, and you were important enough for him to receive you, he'd generally receive you at the center of his web of power.

For this president, that was the Oval Office.

"Mr. President, thanks for rescheduling to meet with me. As you know, it's important."

"I'm aware of that. I've read the documents you e-mailed over."

He nodded toward the laptop on his desk, networked into the White House PROFS system.

"It's obvious that we're faced with a growing crisis that could snowball to major proportions. That's why I've asked the vice president, the secretary of state, and Ross Conejo to sit in. Warren's not feeling well and Bill Blandship's in Europe addressing the World Bank, so Battelstein, the assistant deputy, is on his way up from the Pentagon. He's bringing along Bucky."

Yee paused to accept another cup of strong black coffee from an aide, and eye some appetizing French pastries near the large stainless steel percolator as Vice President Betsy Ross Langford entered the room, with National Security adviser Ross Conejo trailing behind her.

As the group began to seat itself in the customary semicircle of comfortable upholstered chairs facing the president's seat in front of the fireplace, and yellow legal pads were being braced atop knees, chairman of the Joint Chiefs General Buck Starkweather entered with Assistant Depsec Arnold Battelstein.

"You've all gotten quick briefs on why this meeting's been convened—and my apologies for ruining your schedules, by the way—so I'll cut to the chase.

"Hampton Yee's people at CIA shocked hell out of me this morning with the intelligence assessment that had just come in and so wasn't in my morning's NIE."

The president paused and nodded as if making a decision to himself.

"I think I'd just as soon turn the discussion over to the CIA director at this point," he said.

"Hamp, lay it out for us, will you? And let us know how long you think the situation will stabilize before one side or the other uses a battlefield nuke?"

The president sat down and cocked his head as the CIA director looked pointedly away from the French pastries that his better judgment told him were bad for his serum cholesterol. Then he glanced briefly at his notes and prepared to speak.

* * *

"**WAHH-HOOOO! WE'RE GONNA KICK US SOME MUTHA-**fuckin' tango ass today!"

"Shit-yeah! Fuckin-A!"

"Right the muthafuck *on*. Wahh-*hoooo*!"

The rebel yell was sent aloft amid the thunderous knell of twenty Harley-Davidson bikes being kick-started and throttled up. Skull's Howlin' Banshees had even found that practically all the gear they'd stashed on the bikes had lain there untouched throughout the entire seajacking.

Their pistols and sawed-off shotguns, as well as spare ammo, had been found where they'd left it all when they'd driven the bikes into the big cargo hold weeks ago in Galveston, having made the ride down without their wives from Albuquerque to meet the departing ship on its way to Aruba. They'd found their helmets, too. Everything intact and good to go.

It looked like the terrorists weren't all that curious about the bikes. Good thing, too, that those tango fuckers weren't bike people.

All throttled up and ready to roll, Jones gave the signal and the Howlin' Banshees wolf pack roared around the cargo hold in a farewell salute to their former captors.

Weak Link and the others were now under guard in the prisoner cages, their own weapons now in the

---

hands of the contingent of nonbiker "troublemakers" who had stayed behind to hold the fort and to provide backup for their warrior brothers on the move.

Popping bitchin' wheelies and leaving smoking black skid marks on the blacktop deck surface as they roared out of the hold, the bikes screamed through the lowest level of the ship without encountering any resistance. They all had their weapons at the ready and were on the alert for trouble, but there was nobody down there, at least nobody with guts enough to show their face and confront the bad bike brothers man to man.

Minutes later the bikers broke out onto the ship's main deck, the Lido Deck, which, from stem to stern, had two swimming pools, indoor tennis courts, and also boasted an arcade of swank shops and a Las Vegas–style gambling casino.

The earsplitting, skull-rattling, bone-shaking roar of the hogs' two-stroke engines echoed and boomed off the walls as the phalanx of Harleys careened through the spacious main lobby of the *King Albert III*.

STILL NO SIGN OF THE ENEMY, THOUGH.

The Lido Deck appeared to be as deserted of friend and foe as the lowest cargo level from which Skull's crew had come.

The sloping, carpeted ramps that linked all the decks together in place of conventional stairways were wide enough for the hogs to negotiate two abreast.

The ramps hadn't been intended for quite the same use the bikers were putting them to, though. Their original purpose had been to make the 955-foot, 109,000-gross-ton ship fully wheelchair-accessible, but they were wide enough to allow the motorcycles to roll through two abreast.

The same went for all the common areas of the ship, including all of the elevators except those reserved for the cruise liner's staff personnel—all had deliberately been built with extra-wide companionway spaces to accommodate passengers on wheelchairs or motorized scooters.

Riding on the lead cycle, Tim "Skull" Jones was on the move. Jones, founder and president of Skull's Howlin' Banshees Motorcycle Club of Albuquerque, New Mexico, rode in the lead, ready to take the first hit or blow away the first badass muthafucka who crossed their paths.

Fuck, fight, or die, the Banshees were sending some damn tangos to hell today, and that was a natural fact.

This was balls-to-the-wall time.

A once-in-a-lifetime event.

This was a proud moment for Skull's Howlin' Banshees Cycle Club. Hell, it was a proud moment for America, thought Jones. The smell of engine exhaust was sweeter than French perfume. Man, they were going to take this ship over, he thought.

The terrorists didn't stand half a chance. Not a fucking chance in hell. Not when Skull's Howlin' Banshees of Albuquerque, New Mexico, had rubber on the floor and leather on their backs.

And if those tangos expected any quarter from the Banshees, they were sadly mistaken. The Banshees' councils of war, carried out under the noses of the terrorist guards, had decided the matter.

The order of the day was "take no prisoners." Terrorists were to be shot on sight and dumped into the briny deep. The sharks would take care of the rest. Fry their fuckin' asses. Let God sort 'em out.

By this time Skull's Banshees figured that the tangos had to know that the cat was out of the bag. The Banshees were loose and they were loud, putting out heavy metal thunder, just like the words to the Steppenwolf biker anthem.

You could hear the bad brothers rumble all over the damn ship. Sawed-off shotguns were snug in bandolier holsters. The only thing missing were a lot of the brothers' leather chaps and other Banshee regalia. A bro—at least when that bro was a Howlin' Banshee—did not like riding .his hog without his chaps on over his jeans, but that just couldn't be helped.

Somehow, the scam they'd worked for bringing along their guns so they could do some shooting in the exotic foreign countries to which the cruise would take them had been ordained by a higher power.

"Wah-hoooo!" shouted Jones and stretched out his right hand to slap his bro Steve "Mutt" Wilson five. He was glad Wilson was riding right up there with him.

Steve, who was called that because he was tall and lanky like the Mutt in the comic strip, was also called that because he kind of looked like a mangy dog, always unshaven. He was a hell of a pharmacist, though, and owned a chain of drugstores in and around Albuquerque.

Mutt also was a good guy to know when a fellow Banshee needed some more exotic nonprescription stuff you didn't get from a doctor but that sometimes was the best medicine for what ailed a man.

"Yo, Skull, we gonna stomp us some bootie, man!"

"Damn shit right we are—fuckin'-A right!" Jones yelled back, shouting to make himself heard over the roar of the bikes as they circled around the empty swimming pool on the Lido Deck and roared through an arcade of deserted shops.

"Spooky shit, though. Where the fuck are they?"

"Same thing I was thinking," answered Mutt.

The bikes had all stopped now, spreading out around the pool so as not to present a bunched-up target to any lurking terrorist shooters who might have them lined up in their gun sights.

From somewhere down the line, somebody shouted, "Man, the tangos must be balling Monk's ol' lady!"

"Shut the fuck up, bonehead. Monk and me are bros and I might just decide to fix it so you don't ball anything deeper than an ashtray again."

"Fuck you—you mothafuckin' pussy."

"Yo, be cool, bro, or I'll kick your fuckin' ass."

Before the shit fight turned into a free-for-all, Skull did what he had to.

BOOOOO-OOOOOMMMMMM!

The report of the sawed-off Mannlicher sounded like a clap of thunder. Guys either ducked or jumped off their bikes and took cover. Some had drawn their guns and were scouting the overhead balcony area for the terrorists they figured had fired at them.

"Now that I got you assholes' attention, listen up!"

Skull stood atop his bike and shouted at the top of his lungs.

"The terrorists might be surrounding us and setting up Claymores or M-60s or some shit like that, and here you fuckers are acting like a pack of goddamn chimps!"

Skull shoved his Detroit-style Mannlicher into its leather bandolier holster and stuck in his mouth one of the prize Garcia Vega cheroots that had come from the can of a dozen that had also been left untouched amid his gear.

"Now, I want you gentlemen to show some discipline and be cool. This ain't no game. These terrorists are pros, bros."

Skull lit up and took a hefty drag, creaming out the smoke through his flaring nostrils.

"This here cycle club's gonna have all the fighting it can handle once we make contact with them tangos, and we will real soon, so just save the shit for when the fan starts turning. Any questions?"

Skull waited a few seconds. Nobody said a thing. He nodded, stuck the cheroot into the side of his mouth, and saddled back up on his hog.

"Then let's fuckin' roll, brothers!" he hollered, looking back at the bros ranked behind him over his shoulder.

Everybody throttled up their Harleys and roared up the ramps toward the Promenade Deck.

13.

UNDER ATTACK

THE PRESIDENT WATCHED THE IMAGES ON THE TV screen with steadily increasing horror.

He'd made the twenty-mile drive from the capital to Camp David late Friday afternoon for a much-needed weekend getaway of relaxation, horseback riding, and golf.

President Travis Claymore had made the hour-long trip in an unmarked government-leased SUV at the center of a convoy of similar all-terrain vehicles that, like his, also bore no official insignia. The vehicles' occupants included senior White House staff, who, like himself and the first lady, were also getting away for the weekend.

Once en route the president had slowly felt the cares of state dissolving as he began to relax.

Later, after a Swedish sauna and a few ice-cold beers, the president was even considering going so far as to unscrew the cap of the virgin prescription bottle of Viagra that had been given him by the White House physician after a discreet discussion with the first lady and on the advice of the surgeon general.

The first lady also had made it clear to the president that she expected him to try at least one Viagra tablet at bedtime.

The president knew that his wife had been talking to the wife of the Speaker of the House, who had made a total ass of himself by enthusiastically endorsing the aphrodisiac drug in a paid television advertisement. Obviously the Speaker of the House had reason for his endorsement, since what had long been a rocky marriage suddenly became a peaceful one almost overnight.

The president had originally meant to break his promise to the first lady, but now thought differently. It was doctor's orders, wasn't it? To say nothing of a husband's marital obligations. He went to the medicine chest and took out the bottle. He decided to have another beer and placed the long-necked bottle on the side table next to his comfortable motorized plush leather recliner.

The president had on CNN, which was one of the three round-the-clock news programs he habitually watched. He smiled as an errant thought flitted across his mind—he needed to watch something to put him in the right mood for . . . later on. The report on the national retail chain Mall-Mart's selling of controversial bioengineered woolens just didn't cut the mustard.

The president reached for the TV remote and raised it toward the screen; then his jaw dropped. A new report had just come onscreen. The images, the horror —it had all returned.

Hooded terrorist executioners stood over a hooded American hostage. Behind them on the wall hung a familiar flag. A banner of evil.

The president wished he'd never seen it before, but it was instantly recognizable as the tricolor emblem of the Colombian Evangelistas.

A machete was raised as two masked killers held down the victim. As the camera zoomed in, one of the Evangelistas reached down and yanked off the hood. Coils of blond hair spilled out as the hostage raised her head and exposed her face. The camera zoomed in for a tight close-up.

The hostage who was about to die, Claymore

realized with fresh horror, was Heather Hunnicutt, the wife of the secretary of defense.

For an instant or two the camera zoomed in on the face of the victim for an even tighter shot. Heather Hunnicutt wore a strange, almost demented smile—the president had seen it before on the faces of other hostages. She looked like she might have been drugged. Or brainwashed. Or both.

"Speak your words," a voice, muffled, barely audible in the background, said. "Atone for your nation's monstrous crimes and heinous deeds. Death to America! Death to the United States! Death to the Zionists who rule the Great Satan!"

"Yes. I'm thankful for the chance to say these last words," she replied, staring with glazed eyes straight into the camera lens. "I know now I've lived my whole life for this single moment."

Heather Hunnicutt licked her pouty French lips and smiled—smiled almost coquettishly.

"I'm grateful that I'm about to die. So I can show my countrymen, and especially my president, that not all Americans are bad, that not all of us are Zionist stooges. I'm about to give my life to show how sincere I am."

She paused a moment and again the tongue flicked out over the overblown, collagen-inflated lips.

"Please forgive my country for its evil and its sins. I'm ready to die now. Please kill me."

She was really smiling now.

"*¡Mataran!*"

The command, again from behind, and the flash of the machete as the camera lens pulled back quickly to a wide-angle pan.

The blade striking the head.

The head severed by the sudden, ferocious blow, the blood spurting as the head fell to the floor.

A cry of obscene victory as the faceless terrorists hailed the executioner, and then the sudden absence of imagery as the recording suddenly cut off in a confusion of video static and crackling electronic chaos.

The president sat dumbfounded, realizing that his secure phone line was ringing—had to have been ringing—for many minutes before he'd become aware of its sound.

Numbly, he reached out and picked up the handset of the wired, landline phone.

"Yes," he said. "I've just seen it. Yes, terrible, horrible. Words can't describe my state of mind right now. I'm . . . just dumbfounded."

The president paused, listened.

"I concur," he replied. "I want preparations stepped up. This atrocity . . . this abominable, cowardly act . . .

could start a media feeding frenzy. We've got to show the American people—hell, show the world—that we're not just . . . impotently . . . sitting by, watching. We've got to do *something*."

The president's eye strayed toward the bottle of Viagra on the side table. A word wandered into his mind—impotence. He shook his head glumly.

"Right. Keep me posted."

The president replaced the handset in its cradle and leaned into the comfort of the heavily padded recliner.

He stared listlessly at the TV screen with a mind bent on revenge as he thumbed a button on the chair's remote.

"WAHH-HOOOO!"

The Banshees were rolling, gunning their hogs, and shouting out earsplitting rebel yells to lift their spirits and tune their tautly stretched nerves. Each member of the cycle club was aware that pretty soon they'd meet up with the terrorists, and then there'd be a fight. That meant that some of them might not make it.

None of them were fooling themselves—the odds against them were stacked pretty heavy. The bad guys were neither pushovers nor amateurs either.

They were hard cases—well-armed, dangerous hard cases, most of whom believed they were on some kind of insane mission of cosmic importance.

That's not to say that the Banshees were throwaways or pussies either. All of the men riding behind Skull Jones had done hitches in the military, and some had even been cops.

Man for man, bro for bro, each Banshee was more than a match for any damned punk-ass terrorist shit.

It was the odds that made the problem—the quantity, not the quality, of the opposition. There were far more of the tangos than there were Banshees. The tangos had a well-prepared plan, which the Banshees didn't, and the badasses also packed far heavier firepower than the few shotguns and pistols the Banshees had managed to stash away onboard the liner.

Yeah, some might have called the mission suicidal. So be it, then, thought Skull. A man had to stand his ground sometimes, no matter how long the odds or how short the chances. That was part of being a man. And it was *definitely* part of being a Banshee.

The only thing that bothered Skull was the absence of contact so far. Starting from the first and lowest cargo deck, they'd rolled up through seven of the nine levels, of which the Sun Deck was the uppermost.

The broad, carpeted wheelchair-accessible ramps that connected the decks had been their zigzagging vertical highway, taking them up from the cargo deck to the Plaza Deck—the first passenger deck—then to the Riviera Deck with its ball courts, theater, and two swimming pools, then to the Promenade Deck.

The Promenade Deck, called the Dolphin Deck on the *KA III*, was the main interior deck of the cruise liner. This deck, with its broad corridors, also was the widest of the ship's numbered passenger levels, excluding the cargo hold.

Skull had figured that this deck would present the best location for the enemy to stage an ambush and decided to stop the bikes and look around.

"Whoa!"

"You thinking what I am?"

Skull's lieutenant and copresident of the Banshees, John "Stomper" Barlow, leaned back in his seat and took a sip from a flask of Old Number Seven malt whiskey. Stomper passed the flask to Skull, who took a nip, then passed it back down the line.

Other Banshees also had their favorite sipping whiskey on them, and the bikers took full advantage of the break time to have themselves each a little taste.

The corridor quickly filled with the smoke of the

long, slim cigars favored by the bikers, some of which contained more than just tobacco, from the fragrant smells that began drifting through the passageway.

Skull held up his hand and slowed his Harley to a halt. He leaned back and fired up a fresh panatela, thinking for a second.

"I think we ought to split up and look around some. It's odd we haven't shook nobody loose yet. It's like the ship's deserted. How can that be?"

"It can't. I don't like it."

"Me neither."

"Have some of the brothers knock on some cabin doors. See what happens next. Pass it down the line. But remember, they all gotta be cool."

"Right. Don't bust down no doors 'cause they might be booby-trapped."

"Yeah, and also there might be a mothafuckin' tango standin' behind it totin' some heat."

"Yeah, Skull. I gotcha, brother."

"Tell Regan and Busch to case one side of this here deck and Tootsie and Mungo to do the other."

"Right. Yeah. What about the Pineapple?"

"You mean Dole? Yeah, him, too."

Stomper throttled his hog and ran down the line. Pretty soon the four bikes belonging to the guys Skull had delegated peeled off and roared away.

The brothers came back without anything concrete, though.

Skull's crew was about to roll up the next set of ramps onto the next upper deck when they made contact with the first nonbiker they'd seen in hours.

14.

DODGE THE INCOMING

"YO. HOLD UP, BROTHERS."

Something small and dully shining, made of metal probably, had just rolled around a turn in the corridor, then another, and then a third. The things, whatever they were, made a smooth, whirring sound as they moved.

"Looks like my kids' toys," Mooner volunteered.

"They ain't no toys."

Skull didn't like their looks. Then he noticed the little things that looked like webcams mounted at their fronts and swiveling back and forth as the things advanced.

"Blast those fuckers!" he shouted. "They're some kinda bomb bullshit."

Nobody moved. The Banshees were too frozen to act in the moment of crisis.

Taking the initiative, Skull whipped his sawed-off Mannlicher from the hog's side holster and took fast aim at the first of the three little wheelie doodads coming at his crew. The cut-down shotgun bucked in his fist, blowing a fan of 30.06 steel buckshot down the corridor. The ball-bearing hornet swarm chewed into the first little robot like a set of flying dinosaur teeth and it exploded with a single and very loud bang.

"Shit, them's antipersonnel mines!" shouted Stomper Barlow.

"Fuckin' right!" Skull agreed, pumping out the spent cartridge and triggering another salvo of buckshot at the next two remote-controlled robotic mines that were suddenly taking evasive action, dodging this way and that.

The bullpup Mannlicher bucked in Skull's fist one more time, and a second fan of buckshot tore up a lot of carpet and bored a brace of holes in a stateroom door, falling short of its now fast-dodging target, but a third volley snuffed the little smart bomb, too.

That wasn't the end of it, though. Now the word

came down from the end of the line of bikes that more little bomb wheelies were rolling their way in a hurry. Fresh replacements for the antipersonnel robot weapons that had been blasted to smithereens were now also rolling toward the bikes in front again.

At least the brothers didn't need any further instructions about what to do at this point. Bullets flew thick and fast from a bevy of Howlin' Banshee guns, barely drowning out the rebel yells of Skull's biker bros as they whacked the robot mines like clay ducks in a shooting gallery.

It seemed like a long time passed when the brothers realized that the enemy had finally shot its wad. The steady stream of little wheelie bombs had stopped entirely. There weren't any more left, it seemed.

Now one thing was getting pretty obvious, too, at least: the enemy was close. The tangos apparently had used up their little arsenal of remote-controlled weapons, but they surely still had plenty of guns handy. Yep, the terrorists were near at hand, and now only a few decks lay between them and the topmost Sun Deck, which would bring the Banshee posse up from the ship's interior and into the open.

Well, bring 'em on, thought Skull, knowing that each of the brothers felt exactly the same way he did.

"All right, brothers!" Skull shouted, mounting his hog. "You girls saddle up and get set to whack some fuckin' tangos. We are gonna be ready to fight, fuck, or die. Anybody who doesn't want to ride can turn back right now."

There were no takers of Skull's offer. The only sounds he heard were the assorted clicks of ammo being loaded into the chambers of pistols, shotguns, and bullpup automatic rifles, and the glassy clink of Molotov cocktail bottles batting against the metal sides of hot-engined bikes.

"Howlin' Banshees—on my signal—*let's fucking roll!*"

Instantly the din of revving Harley engines made a deafening sound as it reverberated off the walls of the corridor.

The brothers were about to meet the renegades who'd hijacked the ship, and each of them knew they were in for a battle royal as they rolled their bikes up the next corridor toward the deck above them.

"And listen up—we're gonna hit that next ramp single file so we don't bunch up so much," Skull added.

"And we're gonna ride fast and come out into the open throwing bullets like hell."

"What if they got hostages?" a brother shouted.

"We gotta take that chance. One way or the other, there could be casualties. Just try not to hit any friendlies. Any questions, gentlemen?"

There weren't any this time either.

"Then, brothers! It's time to unfurl the Stars and Stripes. We're gonna ride into battle flying the fuckin' colors of the God-blessed United States of America, the greatest nation on earth, along with our club's colors!"

Skull unrolled the flags and stuck them on upright tubular holders on his bike. The rest of the bros all had their bikes outfitted similarly—they'd planned to fly their colors and Old Glory both on the various stops during their month-long ocean cruise vacation. None of them had ever dreamed they'd be flying the colors the way they were about to do now.

Skull's Howlin' Banshees had planned to fly Old Glory as they rode through foreign countries, shooting off their American guns and drinking beer. That plan had been dashed by fate, but the flag was about to fly just the same, and those guns would roar, too.

"Now mount up and let's ride. Fuck the tangos. Long live the Howlin' Banshees Cycle Club! God bless America!"

"Yeah," shouted a brother down the line, "fuck 'em. God bless America!"

- -

A chorus of rebel yells seconded that motion as the bikes revved and roared into battle, the Stars and Stripes flying on each of the Harleys along with the grinning, flaming skull that was the Howlin' Banshees' club emblem.

THE PATIENT IN ROOM 307 LOOKED AT THE BUXOM nurse who had come into the room and placed a paper cup containing an assortment of colored drug tablets onto the side table by his bed. She also placed a clear plastic cup two-thirds full of bottled water drawn from the dispenser by the nurses' station on the table.

The patient regarded the nurse balefully but didn't move a muscle.

"I suppose to watch you taking them," she informed him.

"I don't give a fuck, lady," Warren Hunnicutt told her. "I'll take them later."

"I told you I'm suppose to watch you taking them," she said, using a scolding tone of voice that only infuriated the patient more.

"You're treading on thin ice, young lady," the patient said. "I'm sure you're aware of who I am."

"Yeah, I know you a big shot. I still suppose to watch."

"Be a nice person and leave before I have one of the Marines guarding the door throw you out on your admittedly photogenic ass."

"What you say 'bout my ass?"

"Just leave, would you please?"

The Marines didn't scare her. It wasn't every patient at Bethesda Naval Hospital who had Marines guarding the door, but considering that the hospital had played host to numerous government VIPs in its venerable history, Marine guard details weren't an all that uncommon sight.

"Look, I tol' you. I suppose to . . ."

The secretary of defense watched her eyes and saw her mentally change gears.

She wasn't scared, Hunnicutt decided. She'd just decided that she didn't give a hang anymore.

"All right, you take them later. But I come back and no find you take them I sit on your face."

Hunnicutt bet she might as she turned around and left. He sat there awhile deciding whether he'd like the nurse to do what she threatened or not. Then he reached over and picked up the paper cup, reached inside, and plucked a lozenge-shaped red spansule with Pfizer printed in white on it from the bottom. He dropped the pill back and rattled them all around inside.

Then he got out of bed and padded barefoot into the bathroom. He upended the paper cup over the commode, crumpled the cup, and tossed it into the wastebasket. Then he flushed the john. They had one of those superflushers installed that almost knocks you off your feet and leaves you with the smell of the ocean in your nostrils, the same kind they had at motels nowadays. The commode made short work of Hunnicutt's medications.

The secretary of defense padded back into the room and studied himself in the mirror above the small dresser against the wall opposite the bed. Hell, he looked like shit, he thought. Nevertheless, looks could be deceiving.

He'd awakened to the sound of a sparrow's beak tapping against the window. In the sunlight that had streamed through the slats of the semidrawn venetian blinds, he saw the long shadow of a tiny bird moving jerkily as it pecked at the window.

What the hell is that bird doing here? he thought. His next thought was, *what the hell am I doing here?*

He'd checked himself into Bethesda for treatment for worsening depression since the news of his wife's apparent martyrdom-style execution was shown on global television. The doctors had put him on the usual medications after assuring him that shock treatments were no longer in vogue as a cure-all for mental disorders, and in any case his condition wasn't the kind that would have called for them.

Rest and talk therapy would help him recover. The medical center was discreet. They had experience containing leaks. He'd be out before the media knew about his hospitalization.

Later, a young doctor revealed to Hunnicutt that he'd been placed in the same room in which a predecessor at the Pentagon, James Forrestal, had convalesced.

"Are you sure?" Hunnicutt had asked.

"Positively sure," the doctor had held, sticking to his guns. "The chief medical officer mentioned it and I checked it out on the Bethesda Intranet."

"Were you aware that Forrestal jumped to his death from the window of his room at Bethesda, and so if this is the same room he was in that means he jumped from the very same window in front of which you're now standing?"

The young doctor began looking nervous. He glanced behind him and sidestepped.

"No . . . I didn't. Are you sure about your facts, sir?"

"Do I appear to you to be stupid as well as depressed, young man?"

"Sir, I didn't mean to imply—"

Hunnicutt cut the doctor off. He told him that it didn't matter. Forrestal was Forrestal, and he was who he was. Hunnicutt smiled. It had the desired effect. The doctor took advantage of the moment to beat a hasty exit from the room.

Hunnicutt believed the conclusion of the brief exchange had marked the precise moment of his return to health and sanity, for once again in his life he had lived through a moment that convinced him that Warren Hunnicutt and nobody else knew best for Warren Hunnicutt.

He'd taken only some of the pills the nurse had brought, and only that first day, never afterward. He'd rested most of the week. And then the little bird had awakened him, and Hunnicutt knew that it was time to go back to Washington, back to the world.

He'd weathered many storms in his personal life and career. He'd weather this one, too. He'd be okay. Now he was sure.

Hunnicutt picked up his cell and scrolled down to his secretary's private number. In a moment he was connected.

"I'm checking out of Bethesda," he informed her. "Have my limo ready to pick me up in forty-five minutes."

Hunnicutt listened as he went to the closet and

pulled the hanger with his suit on it from the tubular steel truss rod and flung it onto the bedcovers.

"Yes, I'm feeling much better, but I have to cut you off, Jill," he went on. "I'm coming back, but whether I stay will have to be up to the man who put me there. In short, I want a letter of resignation drafted and ready on my arrival. I'll then ask you to phone the president and ask for a meeting. Should the president prefer that I resign, it'll be all ready for him."

Hunnicutt listened for a minute longer as he sat on the edge of the bed and inspected his shoes, noting with satisfaction that they were still tolerably shined.

"Jill, I hope he doesn't either," Hunnicutt said. "We'll see, though, won't we?"

The secretary of defense snapped shut the plastic clam shell and began to dress. To his surprise, he found that he was whistling. It was from Beethoven's Ninth, as he recalled; the deaf composer's great Ode to Joy.

15.

BATTLE LINES

THE COCOS ISLANDS, KNOWN TO AUSTRALIANS AS THE
Keeling Islands, lie off the eastern extremities of the
Indian Ocean, midway between the Sunda Straits
of southwestern Indonesia and the projecting, needle-
like tip of Western Australia's North West Cape.

It's a part of the ocean that is closely bounded to
the east by four of the United States' steadiest and
strongest military allies in the region—Australia to
the immediate east, Indonesia to the immediate north,
and both India and Bangladesh to the far northwest.
The former of these last two regional powers strategi-
cally controls the Bay of Bengal, which broadens out

into a wide swath of open sea until it meets the Indian Ocean at the equator.

This particular spot on the ocean also places many less dependable allies—and some sworn foes—of the United States in North Africa and the Middle East very far to the west, while to the south there is nothing for thousands of miles except open ocean, speckled with atolls, islands, and treacherous belts of coral reefs.

For this reason, and because of its closeness to the littorals of friendly nations, whose naval and air forces are sometimes called upon to carry out supportive screening maneuvers, it's on the short list of spots favored for conducting highly secret exercises by the U.S. Navy.

Such an exercise had begun today at 0600 hours when the *Euphoria*, a freighter sailing under a Liberian charter that was actually a CIA front, that had departed a U.S. naval installation on the Nicobar Islands before dawn, reached its destination in the waters leeward of the Cocos Islands.

The sea was calm and weather conditions were good, with clear skies overhead and the trade winds blowing gently out of the eastern horizon. As the *Euphoria* reached a predetermined position, the captain ordered the freighter's engines cut.

The two massive screws that had labored to push

----

the battered hulk five hundred miles athwart the long Indonesian coastline shuddered unceremoniously to a halt. The massive steel-hulled vessel came to a dead halt in the choppy waters and began to slowly drift with the current.

The captain picked up the secure, handheld satcom unit that beamed his voice to a Marine colonel stationed on the deck of a stealthy Zumwalt-class destroyer, the *Evanston*, several hundred miles distant from the *Euphoria*'s position. Force One's commander, David Saxon, rogered receipt of the captain's message that the merchant vessel was now in position and ordered the exercise to commence.

All systems were go. Only a short time before, Saxon had received a report that neo-Soviet space surveillance assets—specifically a Gryushkin-class photoimaging satellite bearing the international designator number X07-5455-86 assigned to it by USSPACECOM, the military agency controlled by NORAD, the U.S.-Canadian air-space monitoring agency—had been neutralized.

Key word: *neutralized.*

Not merely blinded—neutralized, for to blind the spysat would have meant that the Soviet GRU and KGB would have known, beyond doubt, that the space-based surveillance platform had been attacked, and

----

from an extrapolation of its orbital position above an area known to be favored by the United States for conducting classified naval exercises, would have suspected enough to have buzzed other intel channels. Before long the NSU would have collected enough intelligence to extrapolate the purpose of the exercise from the given facts.

To prevent this eventuality from materializing, the Gryushkin-class spysat was, as just mentioned, neutralized instead of simply blinded. The neutralization exercise was a joint NASA-CIA-USAF-SPACECOM affair timed to coincide with the scheduled launch of a hyperplane shuttle flight, its mission known by the KGB to be regular maintenance of the International Space Station and military communications satellites in the U.S. Milsat orbital array.

The shuttle mission would, however, place the Gryushkin within range of a single astronaut equipped with a portable flight rig.

The Gryushkin was equipped with proximity sensors, but another covert CIA operation, conducted years before, had covertly obtained the secret clearances necessary to turn off the cameras from ground facilities by remote telemetry.

This task fell to the National Security Agency, which, from its Fort Meade, Maryland, headquarters, temporarily switched off the satellite's proximity sensors.

The blackout, though only minutes in duration, was long enough for a shuttle astronaut to reach the Gryushkin and attach a small field-effect generator module that would simulate main sensor failure for the time needed to conduct the exercise in the Indian Ocean. Afterward the module would be remotely ejected, to burn up as it fell away into the atmosphere.

Both the North American NORAD and its NSU equivalent in Siberia would track the module as it dropped earthward, but the odds against it being noticed as anything other than one of the hundreds of miscellaneous pieces of space debris that plunge into the atmosphere each day was deemed minuscule enough to warrant the risks entailed by the operation.

Screened by the U.S. Seventh Fleet and Indian and Australian naval vessels and aircraft, safe from distant observation from the near fringes of orbital space, classified so tightly as to be virtually leakproof, the naval exercises commenced at 0600 hours as scheduled with the halt of the freighter *Euphoria* in the eastern reaches of the Indian Ocean.

Not by coincidence but by design, the *Euphoria* was of similar dimensions to another vessel that, half a world away, was crawling eastward across the Atlantic and would soon near the western gateway to the Mediterranean Sea, at Gibraltar.

This was the *King Albert III*.

The purpose of the exercise was also the key to understanding the mission for which it had been staged to prepare—a hostage rescue mission on a scope never before attempted by the military or security services of any nation on earth.

The mission's objective was to liberate, without harm if possible, more than twenty-three hundred of the ship's original twenty-five hundred passengers and at the same time to kill or capture all of the heavily armed and, from all indications, well-trained and strongly motivated terrorist hijackers under the command of Carlos Evangelista.

Also within the scope of the mission was the critical objective of stopping the ship before Evangelista could bluff, threaten, or sneak his way into the Mediterranean. It was feared—and with good reason—that Evangelista had a nuclear device onboard and that, once beyond the Strait of Gibraltar, would try to reach the central Med to detonate the nuke.

The DIA had first been alerted by orbital data from SAMOS-IV, a satellite that senses and tracks thermal signatures from earth-based sources of defense interest to the United States and its allies.

SAMOS uses a combination of long-range thermal sensors and synthetic aperture radars to perform its work.

Hot spots are relayed on false-color map displays to the joint DIA-NSA facility at Fort Meade. These data are available to intelligence customers at the Pentagon and Langley. Each color is keyed to a different type of emissions signature, be it infrared, thermal, or in the visible-light spectrum.

Tracked before and after the hijacking, the *King Albert III* showed very different thermal signatures, the most alarming of which were readings indicating heat emissions consistent with those known to be generated by the decay of bomb-grade radioactive isotopes, in this case uranium-232.

Once these data had been confirmed, other intelligence channels were buzzed. The result, cross-confirmed by several intel sources, was the grim realization that Evangelista had managed, through the international terrorist network, to obtain the fissile cores from old Soviet theater nuclear missiles.

Their source, once confirmed, was equally surprising, and was one to which the CIA would assign primary importance on the president's orders—he'd signed a finding as soon as he'd learned the full details.

The bomb-grade cores had originally been part of

those shipped secretly to Cuba in the early 1960s and that had provoked the Cuban Missile Crisis of October 1962. The cores had come from Soviet missiles that had been left behind at secret underground installations in the Sierra Maestra region of Oriente Province, the site where the missile launchers had first been discovered aboveground by routine U-2 spy-plane overflights.

Fissile cores decomposed as the isotopes decayed. The cores eventually grew unusable as explosive materials. The actual warheads were now duds and would produce only nuclear "fizzes," not actual detonations. But Evangelista's plans required only the detonation of a dirty bomb, not a full-scale blast. Once the existence of the nuclear device onboard the *KA III* was known, the rest had been easy to work out.

The Mediterranean Sea flowed between the littorals of two continents. Its waters fed indirectly and distantly into the Persian Gulf, and through the Suez Canal the Med gave access to the Red Sea. The Med was critical to the navigation of the world's oceans, and therefore critical to American commerce and defense. Strike here and you struck a mortal blow against the United States.

The navy also confirmed, by way of the Woods Hole Oceanographic Institution, that the oceanography of the central Med was such that even a small nu-

----

clear blast, if placed properly, could create severe blockages to the free passage of shipping that might take decades to repair, if ever.

Shortly after 0600 hours, as the *Euphoria* stopped its engines as planned, and ground to a halt on the high seas, Marine Force One specialist forces began to converge on the target vessel from a variety of forward deployment locations and by a miscellany of special means.

Some of Saxon's special operators stealthily approached the *Euphoria* from beneath the sea, using two-man SDVs—swimmer delivery vehicles—while a company-strength detail slid beneath the waves in a Seawolf-class attack submarine specially equipped for the stealthy mobilization and covert delivery of Marine special forces personnel.

Still other Marines of Saxon's unit deployed on the *Euphoria* from the air, descending from ropes hung from hovering Seahawk helos, clustered like olive-drab grapes on a monster vine, and firing compact automatic weapons to cover their buddies who were already boots-down on the freighter's heaving deck.

Onboard the freighter was a cross section of the types of personnel and situations that the rescue force would be likely to encounter, based on surveillance data and best guesstimates from intelligence agencies.

Mock terrorists in the all-black uniforms and balaclavas seen onboard the *KA III* patrolled the deck, while mock hostages were confined to various holding areas belowdecks. The operation was planned to take advantage of stealth, speed, and surprise to achieve its multiple objectives and maximize its chances of success.

The results would be carefully analyzed at the Pentagon and especially at Marine Force One's sea base headquarters, where Doc Jeckyll was watching real-time visuals beamed down from an assortment of airborne and spaceborne RSTO assets that included a Global Hawk UAV, a Predator UCAV, and various ELINT aircraft such as AWACS and JSTARS that were orbiting in and around the area of operations.

While the maritime war games were still in progress, the actual cruise liner was being monitored only by an Improved Crystal photointelligence satellite that had been jockeyed into an overhead orbit and was permanently assigned to track the *KA III* throughout the duration of the crisis.

Jeckyll expected surprises to come out of the exercise, but he'd never expected what the real-time imaging telemetry from the Improved Crystal suddenly revealed.

Seemingly from out of nowhere a motorcycle gang had materialized on the *King Albert*'s main deck. The

---

bikers were firing a motley mix of small arms and us-ing homemade Molotov cocktails as grenades against Evangelista's men.

The firefight was brief and brutal. Even as Jeckyll began frantically punching up the location of every manned and unmanned airborne asset that might con-ceivably be brought into position to assist the bikers, the pitched battle was over.

Predictably the bikers had failed in what was ap-parently their bold but reckless bid to take back the ship by force of arms. After the dust settled, some of the bikers seemed at least to still be alive, although the terrorists took to beating the survivors as they were again taken prisoner.

There was nothing left for Marine Force One's chief technical specialist to do but save the video to an MPEG file and put it on the network for his boss, Colonel Saxon, to review along with the other big chiefs and medicine men on the military totem pole.

Marine Force One now at least had something new to factor into its equations, although to Jeckyll it was an open question as to whether what he'd just discov-ered would be a help or a hindrance in the end.

* * *

DAWN REVEALED THE BLOODY AFTERMATH OF THE
firefight that had taken place in the darkness hours
before. Debriefings of survivors from among the
British SAS force that had been assigned to guard
Sector Bravo-Victor of the transbalkan NOVS pipeline
were taking place within minutes of the return of the
Pave Low helicopter that had been dispatched to rescue the special forces commandos in the wake of the
surprise combat engagement.

From the debriefings it quickly became clear that
the SAS troops had been walking their recon perimeter
and scanning the demilitarized zone around the
pipeline sector.

The DMZ was a buffer zone placed by U.N. man-
date between EDF or European Defense Force-held
territory and terrain controlled by NSU forces. It
should have kept both sides deconflicted, but a
friendly sector patrol had run into an NSU patrol that
had somehow breached the DMZ and encroached on
EDF-controlled terrain.

Sector Bravo-Victor was primarily an area of
sparsely forested granite outcroppings, and it af-
forded many ideal positions in which to situate observation posts and establish fire positions for both
sides. Friendly forces and NSU troops alike used
the sector to keep tabs on each other's activities

while the tense, U.N.-mandated stalemate remained in effect.

Sector Bravo-Victor was a cross-border region, too—the petroleum pipeline skirted the Azerbaijani border by only a few feet in some places, though on a map at least its builders had been careful to make sure that every inch of it was planted on Armenian soil, from which it snaked its way overland due south, to Turkey. Here the crude was pumped aboard ocean-going tankers at an offshore transloading jetty.

On one side of the sector were two armored divisions of NATO and European Defense Force troops, mainly British, German, and French—no U.S. or Canadian forces were in the region yet. It was the U.S. position that negotiations take place to prevent what the State Department considered a potential flash point to nuclear war from igniting into a regional conflagration.

On the other side of the sector were at least two, and maybe more, NSU mobile armored divisions— with the elite Josef Stalin Division in front and the redoubtable Leonid Brezhnev Division, less select, but still tough, well equipped, and formidably trained for mobile armored operations behind.

Since the NOVS oil pipeline was a prime bone of contention—the neo-Sovs claimed that it pumped

Armenian slant-drilled oil from under the NSU border, and was therefore pumping oil stolen from Russia to the greedy West—it would be certainly one of the first objectives contended for if the stalemate ever ballooned into a shooting war.

Observers feared that what had happened during the early hours of the morning might make that a stronger likelihood than ever. Which side had fired the first shot was uncertain and probably would never be known for sure.

The Russians claimed that the SAS commando patrol, riding heavily armed special forces buggies that were equipped with .50-caliber machine guns and rocket launchers, had ambushed an NSU foot patrol that had strayed into the DMZ by mistake.

The British claimed largely the opposite, that the SAS had been caught in a well-planned night ambush in which three of the mobile patrols were led by diversionary movement into a kill box—an upslope ambush on a stretch of prepared road lined with phased Claymore-type antipersonnel mines and with a rifle platoon lining the base of the shallow embankments on either side and setting up a lethal cross fire using automatic small arms.

While United Nations monitors riding AFOR (Azerbaijani Force) armored vehicles marked with large white Vs resembling those seen during the Yugoslavian civil wars of the mid-1990s, and also during the fourth Israeli-Egyptian September War of 2019, shuttled across the DMZ between the two armies and statesmen engaged in furious shuttle diplomacy between West and East, increasingly ominous rumbles came from the Kremlin that threatened an imminent escalation should the West not stage an immediate pullback from the DMZ.

The NSU delegate to the United Nations, speaking before the Security Council, made the Kremlin's cease-fire terms clear.

All Western forces, including NATO and EDF troops, were to withdraw to not less than five kilometers from the Armenia-Azerbaijan DMZ. The neo-Soviets did not offer to withdraw their forces in return, however, stating that since it had been the NSU that had been attacked without provocation, the NSU had no obligation to fall back by even one inch.

It was obviously an unreasonable demand designed to provoke the British bulldog—and its allies—into instant rage, and was immediately interpreted as a political follow-on to a staged military operation in which Russian commandos had deliberately "strayed" into the British zone and come into contact with the SAS security patrol.

Whether true or not, the British ambassador replied that if the Russians thought the United Kingdom would agree to such insulting terms they were as mad as some of their former czars and czarinas.

Within an hour, war plans were being drawn up at EDF headquarters in Brussels, Belgium, with the United States desperately trying to pour cold water on the rapidly rising flames of military conflict.

Within sixteen hours of the skirmish, as war clouds loomed ever higher, the world tottered on the brink of a major regional conflict that had every earmark of developing into the long-dreaded final Ragnarok of World War III.

At least that was how the State Department and the White House viewed the developing situation.

This was largely because the United States knew something that neither the British-German-French coalition nor the neo-Soviets and their Romanian and Bulgarian allies believed anyone but themselves knew about.

This was that both sides had violated international treaties and prepositioned tactical nuclear weapons on the battlefield. The nukes were in the form of mobile medium-range missile launchers. They were also present in the form of smaller, short-range weapons such as nuclear artillery shells and even nuclear mortar rounds.

The U.S. Department of Defense had run secret computer war-gaming simulations on what would happen in precisely this region of the world—the Nagorno-Karabakh region—should East and West collide with tactical nukes and a mix of subtactical nuclear weapons.

The simulations never departed from a single outcome.

Full-scale nuclear exchange within forty-eight hours. Regional nuclear exchange within three to five days. Global nuclear exchange a limited but definite possibility within ten days to two weeks.

The president of the United States knew about these ghastly war-gaming predictions. He knew that a clock was ticking and that the world teetered on the brink of disaster, maybe even on the still darker verge of genocide and mass human extinction.

The president was not one to take counsel of his fears, but like Ronald Reagan at the height of the Cold War, he was afraid now, and he took steps required under the Homeland Security Act to preserve continuity of government should the worst-case scenario materialize.

The president signed secret orders that would result in a clandestine mobilization of key national figures to secret underground locations near Washington,

----

D.C., such as the Alternate National Military Command Center beneath the granite fastness of Raven Rock on the Pennsylvania–Maryland border.

The end seemed to be near, and getting closer all the time.

IT WAS ALMOST AT THAT MOMENT THAT A SHAKEN man, hoping for personal redemption, walked from the confines of his room at Bethesda Naval Hospital and glanced at the window from which the first of his predecessors at the Department of Defense had jumped to his death, before climbing into the waiting limousine that was to speed him across the Potomac for a meeting at the White House Oval Office.

16.

SECRET MISSION

IT WAS NOW LESS THAN TWELVE HOURS SINCE
wrought-iron doors of the West Wing entrance to the
White House had pivoted back on their hinges to per-
mit egress to the black Lincoln Continental flying the
secretary of defense's flag. For eleven hours at least
Warren Hunnicutt had no longer held the office in
which he'd been placed at the pleasure of the U.S.
chief executive.

Having arrived at the White House, Hunnicutt's
heart had sunk when the president had accepted
his offer to resign—it was a largely token offer, and
Hunnicutt had hoped it wouldn't be accepted.

It had been, though, and Hunnicutt, when he'd

heard the president's final verdict, began feeling faint. For a moment he believed that he might collapse. Then, through a spinning maelstrom of vertigo, he heard the president's words that cut through the mental fog like a white-hot knife.

"But Warren, I want to give you another job. One even more important. It's a job nobody but you can handle. You can't do it as the defense secretary. You can only do it as my personally delegated troubleshooter. You've got the kind of reputation and global presence that few others can boast of. The leaders of all the principals, from the British to the Soviets and in between, all know you; so do chief military commanders around the world."

Hunnicutt began to interject, but the president silenced him with a wave of his hand.

"Hear me out, Warren. If you accept my offer, it'll be with the understanding that the job will come with unprecedented powers.

"You would have a direct channel to me at all times, bypassing all military, political, and diplomatic circuits. You could negotiate treaties on behalf of the White House. You know about the tactical nukes—you also know about the apocalyptic war-game scenarios.

"No point in mincing words. We're on the brink of disaster. Take the job, Warren. America needs you."

Hunnicutt sat down. He sat down hard, without intending to. It had happened just like that. One moment he was on his feet and the other he was sitting on the comfortable chair in front of the president's desk.

Then he realized that the tears he'd felt welling up in his eyes wouldn't come. Instead there was a sense of quiet strength, of serene confidence, of steely determination.

He could do this job.

"Mr. President, I accept."

"You have no idea how relieved I am to hear that, Warren. I'll place Air Force One at your disposal. There will be no mistake about your mission—by anyone."

That had been most of what had been said. Hunnicutt had resigned from his old job, but he now had a new mission. Within minutes the former defense secretary was back out the West Wing entrance of the White House.

Instead of reentering the limo that had brought him, he got aboard the presidential helicopter, Marine One, for an express flight to Air Force One, which was already fueled and ready for takeoff on a well-guarded landing field at Andrews Air Force Base, southeast of the capital.

Now, some eight hours after the double-decker

747 had taken off from Andrews with a transatlantic flight plan logged into its GPS-linked navigational system and a hastily assembled complement of journalists and media crew accompanying the president's special emissary, Warren Hunnicutt was in another limousine, traveling along the Peripherique ring highway that encircled Brussels. His estimated time of arrival at the European headquarters of NATO was fifteen minutes.

Hunnicutt smiled for a moment, thinking that only a short time ago he'd been a patient at the Bethesda psychiatric wing whose political opponents and the media's oddsmakers alike had given him up for dead.

What a world this was! It never ceased to surprise. *Look at me now,* Hunnicutt thought.

The day was blessed by some of the clearest, finest weather Hunnicutt had ever seen. The tranquil air was limpid, and he faced the start of a mission of supreme importance that could potentially rank with George Marshall's post–World War II plan that forever bore his name.

The best part of it was that Hunnicutt wasn't euphoric. He was centered and focused, aware that as things stood, today might very well be the last day in history in which the sun shone and the air blew clear and crisp across the face of the planet, before an age of radioactive embers, darkness, and perpetual savagery engulfed humankind forever.

Hunnicutt was sane and his thoughts were sharp, and despite everything that argued otherwise, despite the politicians and VIPs whom he knew were at that very moment scurrying to the safety of deep underground bunkers outside the capital and probably under the Kremlin, 10 Downing Street, and elsewhere, too, Hunnicutt felt hope.

The rest of them might already have given up, but he hadn't. Not yet. He realized that something profound had changed within him.

Hunnicutt only prayed that the world would continue turning long enough to find out just what that something was.

THE SEA WAS CALM, TOO CALM, DECEPTIVELY CALM, in the hours that preceded dawn. Carlos Evangelista had no inkling that his place in the catbird seat of world events might be drawing to a swift and violent conclusion.

The sea was as calm as a bitch in a bar in Bogotá before she slaps you in the face, drawing blood with her fingernails, and the Evangelist, looking out over the ocean, was struck with a sudden premonition.

It wasn't a good one. Call it an omen of doom, call it a foreboding of disaster, call it the cold feel of footsteps on one's grave, call it whatever you might, the Evangelist felt a peculiar sensation that was the exact opposite of the one that Warren Hunnicutt was experiencing half a world away.

The Evangelist spat into the sea and turned away from the rail of the ship.

Nothing was wrong, nothing was amiss, he assured himself. The entire cruise liner was his. The American biker gang—they'd been unexpected, but he'd decided to have some fun with them just the same. He'd toyed with them, had his troops play cat-and-mouse games as they rolled their hogs up through the cruise ship's many levels unopposed.

At the top, his men waited in ambush. That had been the end of the cycle club's little mutiny. The survivors were now back in their cages, and the guards who had permitted them to escape had been severely reprimanded. There would be no repeat of their foolish escapade.

Everything was under control. And yet . . . there was this feeling, this flutter in the gut.

Okay, he thought. *No use deceiving myself. Something's coming. I can feel it. Well, fuck it. I'll be ready for it when it* does.

The Evangelist went below, to where the nuclear device was ready for immediate arming.

He knew that preparing it for detonation would make him feel much better. As the Evangelist envisioned the radioactive death cloud spreading across half the global landmass, his heart already began to grow light.

BOOK THREE

A Global Insurgency

What I see is a global insurgency—a global struggle—where a small minority is attempting to hijack and to persuade people to oppose the state system in our world; to oppose civil society, to oppose free systems, not just the United States, not just the West. The attack clearly is against moderate regimes around the world. We see terrorist attacks in the United States. We see terrorist attacks in the Middle East. We also see terrorist attacks in the other parts of the world.

—Secretary of Defense Donald Rumsfeld,
Pentagon press briefing, June 2004

17.

SEA STORM

IN THE FALSE DAWN PRECEDING SUNRISE, ALL THE elements of the long-planned assault on the hijacked cruise liner came together to release the pent-up explosive force of a thermonuclear chain reaction.

Marine Force One's phased assault from sea and air converged on the target vessel in shock waves that came from every point on the compass, using every weapon system and tactical stratagem in their order of battle.

Saxon had hived off the go-anywhere, do-anything sea-air-land force into separate mission-oriented action teams, each of company strength. The MF-1 teams, actually mini task forces, were individually trained to undertake separate segments of the overall terrorist interdiction and hostage rescue operation.

The assault would proceed in coordinated phases, each one dovetailing with the ones that followed and preceded in a building crescendo of operational tempo designed to subject the enemy to successive hammer blows that would crush all resistance.

Each task force was assigned command by one of Force One's tough, battle-tested master sergeants, although as in past MF-1 blitzes, such as those in the Middle East or in South America, each team member was trained and equipped to function autonomously when necessitated by combat contingencies. Each task force also had the option to subdivide itself into two or more combat action squads, subject to the CO's approval. Some, though not all, of the task forces opted for this approach to the mission.

One such hived task force, Team Ripper, was commanded by Sergeant Death, a veteran of many past Force One combat operations.

Ripper was the spearhead of the entire operation. Ripper conducted surface and subsurface operations, converging on the *King Albert III* in two-man buddy teams manning small, sleek, fast Zodiac inflatables above the waves and SDVs, submersible swimmer delivery vehicles, under the water.

Team Ripper's mission was twofold. Its first objective was to secure the liner's hull sections below the water line and to establish a mobile security cordon around the hijacked vessel out to a distance of approximately two hundred meters in all directions.

Once the cordon sanitaire around the vessel had been established, Team Ripper was to immediately prepare for hostile boarding of the ship by follow-on Marine Force One combat personnel. Grapple-and-line climbing gear would be fired from specially modified rifles at storm points across the ship. These had been carefully selected by mission planners at the Pentagon and at Sea Base Alpha, MF-1's maritime headquarters in the South Atlantic.

Drawing close on the surface and beneath it, in craft that were acoustically, visually, and electronically stealthy, Team Ripper's surface contingent halted within eyeball range of the hijacked vessel's deck spaces. Sergeant Death, with the surface attack element, awaited confirmation from the subsurface team that at that moment encircled the *KA III* from stem to stern.

When Death received the two confirmation tones in the earbud of his comms headset, he signaled for the surface team's Blue Man teams—a Marine Force One code name designating sniper squads trained for combat on a one-shot, one-kill priority—to take down the targets they had already acquired during the waiting period.

Almost instantaneously there were the faintly audible clicks of bolt actions of the Mauser sniper rifles favored by the force's Blue Man teams striking the backs of shell casings of 7.62-millimeter full-metal jackets.

There were no other sounds produced by the steel-jacketed bullets exiting the chambers of the specially silenced precision killing instruments. There was only a fleeting chorus of faintly audible metallic clicks sounding softly in the darkness that hovered over the open sea.

A heartbeat later, the dark shapes that had been the standing targets of each of those single bullets dropped out of sight, crumpling to the deck with surprised grunts of pain and terror as the rounds bit into them and shattered into deadly fragments that ricocheted off skeletal bone and ripped apart internal organs, or plunged headlong into the black, cold waters of the open sea.

As the first of the terrorist KIAs dropped down dead, Sergeant Death was on secure satcom to mission headquarters on Sea Base Alpha.

Death confirmed that Team Ripper had established

----

a security cordon around the ship, that climbing tackle was in place, and that first blood had been drawn.

The message was relayed to Saxon, who was en route in the sortie of Seahawk helos that was to form the main corridor of entry to the battle space by Marine Force One airborne commandos.

Saxon confirmed Death's message and gave the order for the second phase of operations to commence.

Stowing his satcom, Death simultaneously ordered his storm cells to blitz the ship via the climbing ropes that now hung from its hull like streams of tears spilling down to the water line, and while Blue Man teams covered their ascent, the first of the commando shock troops to storm and begin retaking the vessel began their combat ascent.

Porting lightweight yet highly lethal Specter submachine guns, the storm cells hustled up the ropes and were quickly engaged in brief, explosive firefights using their automatic weapons, or in hand-to-hand combat with desperate and tough terrorist opponents.

Glowing tracer rounds drew first blood as flash-bang grenades were tossed onto the deck, blinding the tangos and setting them up for the fast, tap-tap death of a bullet to head and heart in rapid succession, or a fast autofire burst at close quarters that stitched open the abdomen and ended life in a moment of horror as intestines uncoiled from bloody cavities and tumbled to the floor.

Green Marines who were mixed in with the force's veterans to be blooded on their first action mission were treated to the bizarre spectacle of their opponents on their knees, trying desperately to stuff their spilled guts back inside open abdominal cavities before they keeled over finally in death.

For the force's veterans there were no surprises left, only another mission to be accomplished.

Soon the first Marines on the floating terrorist Iwo Jima prevailed in first contacts with the enemy and began fanning out across the deck and down into the ship's interior. Then the initial wave of helo gunships and slicks carrying fresh reinforcements began to sweep down on the battle scene like heaven's black vengeance on the blazes of hell.

In the lead slick, just behind the Marine Sea Cobras that were providing air cover, Colonel David Saxon cradled his Specter subgun and looked down on the uppermost deck of the vessel.

For Saxon this time, as every time, it was about to be another case of first boots down.

First boots down, last boots off.

Saxon had never led from the rear.

He wouldn't this time, either.

Close in to the action now, feeling it grow closer by the minute, the scene from the helo's jump deck was one of chaos, flames, and searchlights below as the terrorist hijackers desperately tried to defend against the sudden paroxysmal chaos to which the steamrollering operational tempo of the Marine special force attack had subjected them.

Here and there, two lone men or small groups of combatants locked in fierce death struggles could be picked out from the air. Doll-like figures flailed at one another at close quarters with fixed bayonets, or grappled in a furious tangle of limbs and blur lines of motion. Then there was the sudden cold blue glint of a bayonet or the brief, stuttering flashes of bullets ejected from the muzzle of a gun, and the loser went suddenly limp and slid down motionless in death.

Now, as the first slick drew near to the uppermost sports deck of the *KA III*, and white phosphorous flares seeded from a Hercules flying high overhead suddenly lit up the night, tingeing everything with a flickering white hell-glow, Saxon heard the Sea Cobras' chin-mounted Gatlings begin to angrily thunder as the gunships laid down suppression and covering fire to prepare the ops zone for the airborne shock troops of Marine Force One.

The moments ticked off and then came the drop-master's shout to unass the helo, and it was boots-on-deck time for the airmobile Marine hard chargers.

At the head of the first assault team Saxon came down the line firing his submachine from the hip, feeling solid satisfaction in his gut on seeing the first terrorist he'd killed catch a burst across the heart region that raked him open and almost lifted him off his feet as the heavy-caliber bullets bowled the sucker over backward and sent him landing on his ass, deader than yesterday.

And then Saxon was down, finally down. Landing hard, cushioning the impact under his crouched limbs, he felt the deck rush up to meet the hard soles of his combat boots, and then he was running at a zigzag-ging half crouch, firing from the hip at black-clad fig-ures who darted out of the smoke-tinged hell lights and belched out rotoring stutters of deadly automatic fire from the muzzles of their guns.

Answering with parabellum bursts from the Specter that drew screams of pain, Saxon swept the decks of terrorists, hearing the thuds and battle cries of his Marines going boots-down behind him, and fanning out like him into the chaos of battle while the deafening clatter of the helos' spinning rotor blades and scream-ing turbine engines ascended from the violence on the deck into the flickering insanity of the night, their mission ended, their presence for the moment no longer needed.

As Saxon took cover behind a bulkhead to avoid a hail of terrorist bullets, he drew back and smiled as he listened to the squawk in the earbud of his lightweight communications headset. Reports coming in on Marine Force One's tactical comms net were constantly being received. Each told of the terrorists losing ground while Colonel Saxon's Marines steadily advanced through the reaches of the ship, retaking the cruise liner in record time for a complex, risk-laden op.

Now the suppressing fire from the hidden terrorist's gun started up again. Saxon stuck the end of his weapon out beyond the corner of the wall and triggered off a long burst of automatic fire. It was answered immediately by a burst from the terrorist's gun.

By the familiar sound of the weapon, the hijacker shooting at him was packing a bullpup Krinkov AKR, a good weapon in the open but not the best of choices in confined spaces such as the innards of a cruise ship. Though compact, the Krinkov was still too big and too heavy a weapon. What you needed was a shooter that was light and portable, controllable yet lethal. Saxon's Specter SMG fit all the requirements to a tee.

Saxon decided to take a calculated risk to draw the

hijacker into the open and end the stalemate. Reaching into the side pocket of his fatigue trousers, he extracted a mini-Stingball stun grenade. He pulled the pin and flipped it into the corridor. It arced across the deck, bounced once, and began to roll toward the terrorist's hiding place.

Seconds later the flash-bang went off with dazzling bursts of blinding light and deafening concussive reports. Right behind it, Saxon broke from cover. The Stingball had produced its desired effect. It had flushed the terrorist from hiding and set him up so Saxon could mow him down.

Down the corridor's narrow steel tube a threshing figure clad all in black was limned in the dull yellow light of a mesh-caged bulb that swung from a short chain at the hub of a connecting corridor a hundred meters down. A burst of light flashed from the end of one upraised limb, but the vagrant shots went wild. The terrorist was blinded and his ears rang like firehouse bells.

Saxon's opponent leveled the weapon again. Ready to blind-fire down the companionway, he was obviously prepared to go for broke, to risk blowing all the bullets left in the clip on one last roll of the dice. He never got that far. Before the hijacker could yank the trigger of the bullpup Kalash, Saxon raked him across the belt line with a salvo of 9-millimeter bullets, and the terrorist went down, landing hard, with Saxon hustling fast down the narrow passageway.

Reaching the prone, blood-soaked figure, Saxon crouched, placed his gun muzzle against the figure's head. The hijacker didn't move. He appeared to be dead. Dead was good, thought Saxon. He'd danced to the music and now he'd paid the piper in his own coin.

Down on one knee, Saxon pulled the balaclava from the corpse's face. It was a young face, as he'd expected, but youth was no excuse for murder and kidnapping. You sowed the wind and you reaped the whirlwind. Soon that face would be a grinning skull.

Saxon dropped the tactical face mask to the floor that continued to pool with dark arterial blood. The terrorist KIA awaited a body bag while Saxon's boots rang on the deck of the passageway as he ran deeper into the liner's steel bowels, and slammed a fresh high-capacity clip of 9-millimeter hollow-point bullets into the mag well of the Specter.

18.

FINAL GAMBIT

ELSEWHERE ON BOARD THE *KING ALBERT III*, CARLOS Evangelista also was on the run, but unlike Marine Force One's commander, David Saxon, he was running from—and toward—disaster.

Running to commit the final, unspeakable atrocity.

Running to kill and maybe to die, but if dying, then to take many others with him into the gaping jaws of dark eternity.

Echoing alike through the carpeted, wood-paneled companionways and recreation rooms for cruise vacationers, and the drab steel walls of the crew passageways deep belowdecks like the roar of a many-headed beast of prey, there came the multiple tumults of simultaneous firefights.

Screams, shouts, loud thuds, and muffled booms of explosions whose force made the steel beneath his feet flex and shudder like something alive and terrified, and almost made him stumble and fall, chased the terrorist chieftain like hell dogs sniffing carrion on the wind.

Evangelista bit back the steadily climbing panic that tasted of charred aluminum foil on the back of his mouth, swallowed the mounting fear that made his eyeteeth ache, nerved himself for the difficult tasks that lay ahead, and ran on through the ship's winding metal bowels.

Dominating all the other thoughts in his mind was a single and supremely powerful obsession.

Trigger the nuke, then get away.

The nuclear device was armed but could be set for timed detonation. The *King Albert III* would evaporate in a nuclear mushroom cloud, but the Evangelist wouldn't be on board.

Evangelista had his getaway all worked out. The key to the escape plan was a one-man speedboat that nestled in a specially modified compartment just above the water line in the stateroom formerly occupied by the U.S. defense secretary's wayward wife.

The speedboat, a twin-engine, 750-horsepower Cigarette equipped with two specially modified Mercruiser outboards, could do better than one hundred knots. Nobody had anything comparable. The thirty-eight-foot power boat, a retrofitted Wellcraft Scarab KV formerly the property of a drug runner who'd never been caught, was one of a kind.

The stateroom in which the Cigarette was stashed had been chosen because it was well situated near the liner's stern for a fast getaway. More importantly, the triple-length balcony that adjoined it was an ideal point from which to lower away. He'd had motorized davits installed and could winch down the boat clear to the water line in minutes with the push of a button.

Evangelista was certain there were maritime patrols in the vicinity—soldiers or cops in small, fast power launches and probably helicopters, too, on the lookout for escapees and stragglers—but the situation on board the *KA III* was still chaotic, and he was confident he could slip away undetected. Once in open ocean, the Cigarette had the advantage of speed and range over any and all potential pursuers. All they'd catch was a blur of motion as he sped away across the sea.

There was a strong chance he might make it to Lisbon, and if he could, there was a good chance he could disappear permanently.

Evangelista had friends in Lisbon and nearby Marrakesh, south near the Atlantic coast of northwestern Africa, and more importantly he had access to a lot of money in numbered Swiss accounts. Cash was always the best motivation to get his friends to help him vanish, and cause even his enemies to turn a blind eye. The liner's last charted position made it within a few hundred miles of Portugal, with Spain at its back to the east. If Lisbon wouldn't work, and Marrakesh was closed, then Barcelona or Madrid might still be open.

Yes, he would make it. Certainly he would make it now. Evangelista could feel hope blossom within him, its thriving roots pushing aside the black dirt of fear.

THE TERRORIST CHIEFTAIN WAS OUT OF BREATH when, minutes later, he'd navigated the maze of corridors on the maintenance deck below all the others and found the locked service cupboard—actually a steel closet-sized room used for storing equipment—in which he had hidden the nuclear bomb.

His hands were sweating as he tapped out the access code onto the lighted keys of the cipher lock keypad with which he'd outfitted the cupboard's door.

As he tore open the door, Evangelista felt a surge of triumph.

Game over, he thought.

He'd win after all—had already won, in fact. He was only seconds away from arming the nuke for detonation. Once armed, any attempt to tamper with it would set it off. The liner was as good as radioactive toast.

As Evangelista stepped inside he suddenly became aware of how quiet everything was down here in the ship's deep hold. The sounds of battle were far removed from this lonely place. They were killing each other elsewhere, but down here he had plenty of room, plenty of time, plenty of everything he needed to make victory complete.

He paused for a second and savored the rare moment. There were times in life when a man could almost feel the heavy gears that turned the fulcrum of the cosmos move a notch or two. This moment, Evangelista knew, was one of those extremely rare occasions.

In less than a minute he would unleash a chain reaction of death and chaos upon the world that would reverberate down through the corridors of history and make the carnage of September 11 and Strike Day combined appear tame by comparison.

Others only talked about changing the world. He was about to act. He was about to force the world to change, whether it liked it or not.

Evangelista strode into the steel-walled room. The nuclear device gleamed a dull silver in its specially built shockproof harness. An alphanumeric keypad near its upper end awaited the arming clearance sequence. A new page in history was only a few keystrokes away.

His confidence vanished like mist as he heard the hard, furious cadence of combat boots drumming out a martial rhythm on the steel deck plates of the passageway beyond the open door of the room.

Evangelista pivoted and saw retribution in human form chasing him down as David Saxon stopped, whipped up the muzzle of his Specter submachine gun, and launched a parabellum burst of hollow-nosed automatic fire from groin level.

Evangelista was fast on his feet, luckier than fast. Saxon's quickly aimed SMG burst hit wide of the mark, the brace of bullets sparking as they ricocheted off the bulkheads with the sound of marbles peppering concrete. For the Evangelist, it was the sound of death averted.

Evangelista drew his Uzi machine pistol from his

fast-grab chest holster as he pivoted, took cover around the bend in the connecting corridors, pointed the shooter and snapped off multiple three-round bursts from the compact automatic weapon.

This time it was Saxon who took hasty cover behind the projecting rim of a watertight compartment bulkhead, hurriedly putting a solid inch of tempered plate steel between himself and his enemy's gun.

Stalemate . . . for the moment. Saxon checked his Specter's high-capacity clip and, breathing hard, began to reload the hot clip from a bulging pocketful of rounds on his BDU trousers.

"What is your name?"

The voice sounded out across the companionway spaces separating the two lone combatants, echoing off the steel walls of their metal cage.

"Saxon."

"What is your rank?"

"Colonel. U.S. Marines."

"I am impressed. I am used to being shot at by mere privates."

"My leathernecks have taken the ship, Evangelista. The game's over."

The sound of Saxon's reload snapping into place in the Specter's mag well put an exclamation point to his shouted words. His tone had been harsh, his words

----

curt. He had no time or inclination to palaver with his enemy, only to kill him or to capture him.

"No, not over yet, Colonel. You see, I have three cards left to play. The first is a remote-control unit that I am programming as we speak. Unfortunately for you, Colonel, we're close enough to the bomb for the remote unit to be in range. Once set, the nuke will detonate after a timed delay. My other two cards are a hand grenade that I'm about to toss at you, and this watertight bulkhead right behind me that I will shut and dog down tight as it explodes.

Evangelista punctuated his remarks by a long, stuttering salvo of bursts from his Uzi that emptied the weapon's high-capacity clip. The fast-cycling rounds would force Saxon back into cover and make him shy away from making a break into the open long enough for Evangelista to keystroke in the detonation code sequence and be gone.

"Good-bye, Colonel."

He reached for the fragmentation grenade and prepared to hurl it, and then duck behind the protection of the watertight hatch and swing it shut behind him.

Evangelista didn't hear the rustle of cloth to one side until the highballing runner dived down the passageway and hit him with a flying tackle.

Locked together, the two antagonists rolled on the

floor like fighting tomcats, spilling out onto the twenty-foot-square hub formed by the convergence of three corridors.

Saxon saw the figures struggling on the deck and stepped into the open. He tried to draw a bead on Evangelista with the Specter, but it was impossible to take accurate aim. Saxon couldn't fire for fear of killing the unknown man wrestling with the terrorist. He didn't know who he was, but he was on the side of friendly forces. Until he had reason to believe otherwise, Saxon would treat him as an ally.

Suddenly a knife flashed, swung a vicious half circle in a blur of savage speed, and then there was a muffled explosion. One of the two thrashing figures on the floor rolled away, crying out in mortal pain.

The other lay already dead, with the hilt of a combat knife projecting from the center of his throat and his eyes staring sightlessly into the mirrored black depths of hell.

Saxon ran toward the terrorist's corpse and kicked aside the small device clutched in fingers curled by the spasms of death. To his relief he saw the words "Enter detonation codes" instead of "Final countdown" on its small LCD screen when he stooped to pick it up. Evangelista had not yet initialized the nuclear device.

The ship, his men, and thousands of passenger hostages still alive and about to be liberated would not die.

Then he knelt beside the man who'd assaulted the Evangelist.

He was still alive, but Saxon had seen enough combat wounds to know that the ragged hole in his belly, and the smell of hot grenade shrapnel still cooking off in his guts, and the fringe of charred, blackened-purple flesh around the gaping abdominal slash constituted a death sentence that could not be repealed by any combat medic on earth.

"Tell 'em for me, brother," the hand that clutched Saxon's collar was still strong as iron, and for the moment the blue eyes still held cold fire. They'd killed his bros but he'd escaped a second time, leaving one of the guards a dead man in his place.

"Tell 'em the Banshees did the fucker."

"I will, my friend," Saxon promised, and then he saw the spark of life fade from Skull Jones's eyes.

19.

AFTER-ACTION BRIEFING

THE NIGHT HAD PASSED AND THE SHOOTING WAS finally over. The hostages had been freed and the terrorists were either dead or lying facedown in a heavily secured area in the parking lot of the cargo deck in the cruise liner's deep hold, awaiting the Marine Sea Stallion helicopters that would shuttle them away to prison cells at Guantánamo and similar Black Holes of Calcutta where the United States stashed captives taken in the perpetual, grinding, and always savage war against the global terrorist nexus.

Seahawk medevac helos loitered on ship decks, their main rotors revving slowly as dying and wounded

----

were loaded aboard and then shuttled to the *Kittridge*, a navy hospital ship where a team of combat surgeons was already busily attending to the first triaged cases, and where a morgue detail also waited to photograph, tag, and bag the remains of those who didn't make it back alive.

In fact, body bags were already being borne from the *KA III* on some helo runs, while other choppers ferried in the first of the embedded media contingents who were already filing news reports on their way down onto the retaken vessel.

Still other aircraft, flown by commercial interests and bearing the corporate logos of TV networks and maritime insurers, hovered as close as they dared get before navy gunships chased them off.

More secret operators, members of spook agencies that included the DIA, CIA, and NSA, arrived by way of Seawolf submarine and were hoisted aboard on bosun's chairs on the ends of motorized winches, screened from view by the timely arrival of a frigate dispatched for just this purpose.

The shooting was over.

Now the media circus had begun to pitch its tents and send in the clowns.

* * *

SOMETHING HAD CHANGED. HE DIDN'T KNOW WHAT yet. He couldn't identify the signs, couldn't say exactly what they were. Only he knew that changes had come. Even in the darkness and the cold of his hiding place he could detect that things were somehow different aboard the vessel.

He'd lost track of the hours, lost count of the days, but during his time in hiding he had developed almost a sixth sense concerning the patterns of activity in the spaces of the ship surrounding his self-imposed prison.

Yes, something had changed, because those patterns were no longer the same as they had been, hour by hour, day by day, and week by week since the terrorists had hijacked the ship on the high seas and he had run to the one place where he knew he'd find safety.

He stood, listening carefully in the darkness. Now it was so quiet he could even hear his heart beating inside his chest. In the darkness his senses had become ultrasensitive, ultrasharp. He was certain now. A change, a profound change, had finally come over the ship. Moreover, he thought he understood the nature of the forces responsible for that change—the *King Albert III* had been retaken. Rescuers had stormed the liner, had killed the terrorists on board, had freed the hostages.

That meant that he, too, was now free.

He almost couldn't believe it. It had been so long
since he'd first taken cover from the torture and death
visited on the ship's passengers and crew during the
crisis. But it had to be true. The changes had come.
He could feel them.

It was time to break from cover.

The compartment beneath the engine room had
been originally built to house a lubrication subsystem
for the enormous propeller shaft, but the subsystem
hadn't been installed as the shipyard struggled to
complete the ship within the time frame for its completion bonus. Over a million dollars had ridden on
that completion date being met, and in a secret conference it was decided that the subsystem wouldn't
be installed after all. The ship could operate for years
before anyone would notice. Leaving it out would
shave off the vital days needed to meet the deadline.

The chief engineer had told him about the empty
compartment, as big as two staterooms put together.
The chief engineer was drunk at the time and was
talkative and boastful. They'd been playing cards and
it was late at night. They'd both had a lot to drink.

The engineer had pulled out his laptop and shown
him the plan of the ship, pointing out that officially the
compartment wasn't there—it had been deliberately
left out of the plans by the builders. The engineer had

never explained how he'd known about it, but he'd shown it to him that same night. He'd installed a light inside the compartment, and he flipped it on as they both stepped inside. Nobody but him, he'd said, knew of its existence.

He'd boasted of the uses he'd put it to on the liner's past few voyages. He'd stashed women away in there, whores from the docks of Valparaiso and Panama City, from Marrakesh and Cairo and a dozen other places. He'd hidden drugs and consumer electronics in there, too, to sell at high markups in distant ports of call. It had made him a lot of money. And now, he'd said, there's nothing but these cartons of gourmet food and fine wine. That's all he was carrying on this run. But it would fetch him a pretty penny once they docked in Lisbon. He'd broken out some of his wares and they'd feasted on caviar and French champagne.

Now, alone in the darkness, the stowaway recalled how at the first sign of attack he'd run for the shelter of the chief engineer's secret hideout and bolted the door behind him. He'd expected to find the engineer down there ahead of him, but he'd never shown up. Probably he'd been killed along with hundreds of others. The light had gone out a few days after he'd taken shelter, plunging the compartment into darkness, but the food and drink were plentiful. He'd easily survived.

Now, though, it was time to leave. Slowly he opened the door into the passageway beyond. Above him he could hear the steady throbbing of the ship's engines, and although the light was dim here, it seemed overly bright to his unused eyes. He moved slowly, carefully along the narrow steel tunnel, planning to make his way up through the levels of the ship until he reached the first open deck. He rounded a bend and stopped in his tracks.

Someone else was ambling toward him from the other end of the corridor at a slow, steady pace. He smelled the odor of cigarette smoke. He saw the uniform, and his fear turned to gladness. He'd been right—rescuers had stormed the ship and freed the hostages. Now he was safe.

He stepped forward and took three bullets right in the gut. Coughing blood, he sank to his knees before another burst tore away the crown of his skull. The Evangelista with the subgun sucked on the cigarette between his lips and looked down at the corpse twitching in a pool of crimson, noticing the letters of a word embroidered on the dirty, bloodied rag that had once been a shirt. With the tip of his combat boot he turned the corpse on his back.

Security.

That's what was written on the shirt.

The terrorist let the corpse roll back over and lit another cigarette as he continued down the corridor at his slow, ambling pace. The fighting was far above his head, on the upper decks, and the ship was very big. Maybe if he found a place to hide, he could slip away later, once she put into port. The Evangelista continued along the passageway, searching for a good spot to hide.

"COMING, COLONEL? WE GOT ROOM TO SQUEEZE you in."

Saxon didn't bother to answer. His gunmetal gray eyes surveyed the aftermath of carnage on the deck with all the passion normally contained in two polished camera lenses.

Years of witnessing battles and their aftermaths had permanently given him a thousand-yard stare.

Virtually every square inch of the mammoth cruise vessel bore scorch marks, bullet holes, or pockmarks, gouges, and dents from shrapnel strikes.

Thick, acrid smoke clouds still billowed from interior spaces where things continued burning and fires could, for one reason or another, not be put out yet.

The *King Albert III* would not see vacation action on the high seas for a long time to come, if ever again, mused Saxon. Who in their right mind would take a cruise on this hell boat after what had happened to it?

"Colonel, we gotta leave. You coming or what, sir?"

Saxon shook his head in silent answer and walked away from the shipboard helipad. At his back he heard the chopper's side compartment hatch trundle shut and the helo's turbines begin to rev up to full power with a banshee scream of unleashed, naked thrust that soon whipped round the four-bladed main rotor on top into a flat disk of blurred circular motion.

Fierce prop wash now blew his hair around and whipped his sweat-soaked, bloodied fatigues around his legs as Saxon walked over to the railing and leaned across over the gray-green drink.

The colonel looked out over the dark oceanic waters, his eyes scanning the far-off pencil line of the distant horizon with a vacant look that mirrored the sudden emptiness that had seized hold of his soul.

It took a few seconds more to realize that the muffled sounds behind him were indications that another human being had been speaking to him.

"Colonel, I'm glad I found you."

It was Doc Jeckyll.

He had a satcom phone in his hand.

"It's the president, sir. He says he wants to congratulate you personally."

Saxon stared at the phone with a look that might have been combat fatigue or distaste or both or neither.

Finally he took it and held it near, but not touching, the side of his face, and began to mouth the first words he'd spoken in several hours that had not expressed the icy threat of death.

SPECIAL U.S. ENVOY WARREN HUNNICUTT ORDERED the first of what he planned would be several very dry Beefeater martinis as he settled into the indulgent cushions of one of the prime seats on board Air Force One and unfastened his seat belt.

A shot glass full of meaty green olives that rested on an embossed paper napkin was positioned on a tray within easy reach of his right hand.

The jumbo jet had just leveled off at forty thousand feet. It cruised above western European airspace on the first leg of a transatlantic flight across the polar route that would then swing it southward along the Newfoundland coast about ten hours later on its return to D.C.—shaving off travel time by landing at Dulles instead of the currently air traffic–congested Andrews, from whose runway it had originally taken off.

Hunnicutt sipped the distilled grain alcohol, telling himself that this was one martini he deserved. He'd consider it a toast, in fact. But a toast to what?

He thought it over for another second or two. The answer, when it came, seemed obvious in hindsight.

"To the survival of the human race," he intoned softly, adding, "undeserving as it so often is."

Before the aircraft entered U.S. airspace a bilateral cease-fire and withdrawal would have come into existence between the Europeans and the neo-Soviets. Their contending armies, poised on the brink of potentially annihilative conflict, were now deconflicting.

Negotiations would replace bullets. Jaw-jaw, in Churchill's phrase of long ago, would, for the time being at least, replace war-war.

Hunnicutt had already spoken to the president via secure satellite videoconferencing. He knew he would continue to play a significant role in the arena of statesmanship that was to follow the East-West military standoff in Nagorno-Karabakh.

His was a personal victory as much as a statesman's coup de main. Hunnicutt felt reborn. He counted for something again.

The White House special envoy finished his drink slowly and looked up to see one of the flight attendants hovering silently next to his seat.

The media retinue in back wanted interviews, he was informed. Hunnicutt considered having the message relayed back that he was asleep, but thought better of it.

"Tell them I'll be there to speak to them in a few minutes."

He sat collecting his thoughts before rising from his comfortable seat, trying to mentally draft his main talking points. Sometimes it was harder than at others to get the old bean working, he mused.

Hunnicutt decided he'd just open with a joke and wing it from there. That usually warmed everyone up. He had a good one, come to think of it. One he didn't think they'd probably heard yet.

Hunnicutt wiped his eyeglasses clean with the handkerchief from the breast pocket of his suit, neatly folded and replaced the handkerchief, and rose to his feet. Straightening the knot in his tie, he walked confidently down the aisle to meet the press.

20.

A SURPRISING TURN

FATE HAD GRANTED THE SHARK OF TRIPOLI A RING-
side seat for his own funeral.

His office in the presidential palace occupied the
highest point amid the cream-colored limestone bluffs
that overlooked the Mediterranean, and from its picture window high above the ocean he could now see
clearly with his naked eyes what had just minutes before been visible only with the assistance of powerful
binoculars.

The American armada was drawing closer and
closer to Libyan shores. The U.S. warships already
crowded out the horizon, like a floating city painted
battleship gray. American fighter aircraft, air force

F-22s and naval F-35 Joint Strike Fighters, had long since cleared the skies over Tripoli of Libyan defensive fighters, and now the first wave of V-22 Osprey tilt-rotor convertiplanes were buzzing the presidential palace itself.

Al-Sharq had even tried calling out his two prized Berkut stealth fighter aircraft on the suicide nuclear bombing raid against American military forces in the Gulf of Sidra that he had earlier shied away from. This time there had been no waffling on the dictator's part, no holding back, no last-minute recall—and no further qualms about the Berkuts' tactical nukes blowing the U.S. Sixth Fleet out of the water.

Nevertheless, he'd had a gnawing premonition of defeat even before he'd ordered the planes to launch the mission.

Minutes turned to hours after the Berkuts, Russian for Golden Eagles, had taken off and the twin mushroom clouds that al-Sharq had looked for in vain to tower angrily above the sea, and the wreckage of the destroyed carrier battlegroup, had all infuriatingly failed to appear.

An aide later came in bearing the grim news that nevertheless did not surprise him at all—the Berkut pilots had defected, planes and all.

Both of the advanced Soviet stealth fighter aircraft

were now securely in U.S. hands behind a security cordon at a U.S. naval base on Malta.

Al-Sharq picked up the custom-crafted Colt semi-automatic pistol with the specially engraved pearl handles that he wore at ceremonies. He had laid the pistol across the massive desk of polished Sudanese hardwood, gorgeously inlaid with ancient Bedouin script.

The Shark had intended to use the handsome weapon to blow out his brains when the moment of total defeat was no longer in doubt and capture by the Satanic forces of America was inevitable. The Shark had sworn they would not make another Saddam out of him.

In the end he couldn't bring himself to pull the trigger. He put down the gun and shrugged. He was a coward, but so be it. Instead of using the pistol, he decided to walk one last time through his sumptuous palace.

The spacious marble corridors that had always bustled with palace personnel were now completely devoid of activity. His staff and his generals alike had deserted en masse. Worthless curs, every one of them, thought the father colonel. His footsteps echoed along the polished terra-cotta floors like the furtive tappings of a vagrant ghost.

Grown tired of his final promenade, the Shark of Tripoli trudged wearily back to his office as he heard the ominous, steady martial drumbeat of American helicopter rotors and the wail of turbojet engines.

Soon he heard the echoing, grating noises of heavy military vehicles stopping in the parking areas below, and the sound of many boot-shod feet, rushing swiftly up the stairs and spreading out through the palace's interior.

Al-Sharq sat stolidly at his office desk, awaiting the inevitable. Again his eyes fell to his pistol, but he decided that the stain of his shed blood would mar the perfect beauty of the palace architecture. Such a tragic waste would not at all suit the prestige of a leader of his excellence and refinement.

Instead of eating a bullet, he took an address book from the top drawer of his desk and memorized the names and phone numbers of the best American trial attorney team that oil money could buy.

Suddenly he heard footsteps in the anteroom beyond his office door. He looked up and saw a familiar face. Al-Sharq smiled. He saw in that face that salvation was surprisingly close at hand.

"Saidal Fagih."

The plotter from among the father colonel's inner circle of advisers should have been in chains. The fact that apparently he was free gave al-Sharq hope.

"You're supposed to be in prison, Saidal."

Fagih didn't answer. His muteness had a lot to do with the muzzle of the silencer-equipped pistol that was jammed into the nape of his neck. The man, taller by half a head than Saidal, who stood behind him and grasped the pistol also had been responsible for freeing the rebel government minister.

Al-Sharq recognized the American spook. He had good cause to take heart now. It had been the spook and the secret cabal deep in the heart of the U.S. intelligence community that had placed him in power and helped keep him strong through the years. Al-Sharq had never divined Rempt's true motives or purposes. All he'd known or cared about was that Rempt and those he represented had helped him stay alive through thick and thin. Most importantly, they seemed to continue to want to do so.

"Mr. Rempt," he said. "How good to see you."

"The same," answered Rempt, his long, skull-like face breaking into a diabolical smile. "Did you know that Saidal and you are almost physically identical? Same bone structure. Same general facial characteristics. Same ratio of limb length to torso length. In some ways, in fact, Saidal could be considered . . . your twin."

The two muffled, high-pitched *snit-snits* of bullets exiting the muzzle of the silenced pistol came as no surprise to al-Sharq, nor, for that matter to their victim, as Saidal Fagih slid to the floor.

Al-Sharq watched dispassionately as more bullets obliterated all signs of Saidal Fagih's facial features and dental work. He watched with growing respect for the spook's operational expertise as Rempt poured a powerfully corrosive acid on Fagih's fingertips and palms, to make conclusive identification of the corpse impossible. As he worked, Rempt told the father colonel to gather up whatever few belongings he could carry and come with him. Rempt was getting him out of there to a safe haven.

Al-Sharq glanced at the address book on the desk he'd been leafing through just before Rempt brought in Saidal. The father colonel decided he didn't need it anymore. After all, when you had friends you could count on, who wanted lawyers?

He got up and, at Rempt's instructions, began stripping off his splendid white dress uniform. Rempt was already crouched over Saidal, trying not to get too bloodied as he stripped him to his skivvies.

THE PRESIDENT HAD HASTILY READ THE PAGES handed him by the chief White House speechwriter, trying to focus on the typescript through bleary,

----

bloodshot eyes connected to a weary, distracted brain. His voice and actions showing the tiredness he felt, he'd suggested changes and deletions and then had handed back the double-spaced pages en route back to Washington.

He'd heard the rapid clicking of laptop keys as the speechwriter worked to polish up the draft, thinking that it was a delight to be back in the sunlight again after spending the last eight-odd days in the wretched confines of the secure underground facility beneath Raven Rock Mountain.

The president detested the heavyweight responsibilities of being the one man designated by constitutional law to address the millions of U.S. citizens doomed to nuclear destruction aboveground in the event of a WMD attack. He wished there was a way to save everybody, but that obviously wasn't possible. The most that could be done in the event of nuclear or other WMD-caused disaster would be to salvage the best and the brightest to continue the human race.

This, of course, had to include America's key leadership, such as himself, the vice president, and chief cabinet members. Fortunately, the contingency of surprise WMD attack was now over, hopefully over forever, thanks in large part to the efforts of his special envoy. Of course, it had been the president's own keen judgment and intelligence that had really saved the day, the president told himself, but modesty would prevent him from saying anything on the subject. He'd let Warren Hunnicutt hog all the credit. A president had to control his ego—it was part of being presidential. When he wrote his memoirs he could tell it all, but not while he was still in office.

Now the president stood before the cameras behind the podium on the low stage of the White House press room. At the appearance of the red light on camera one, he looked down at the paper copy of the prepared speech on the lectern, then looked up at the electronic copy on the TelePrompTer screen below the camera and began to read from the text. He'd memorized most of the words, of course, but it was better to have it all in front of you.

"My fellow Americans," the president began, using his customary greeting.

"I stand before you breathing easily again after the dark times of the past few terrible days."

He went on gathering speed, hoping he sounded as presidential as he looked in the video monitor.

"I breathe easily because a Gorgon's head of international crises—any one of which might have spelled grievous trouble for our great nation—has been lopped off."

The president cleared his throat, glanced down at the lectern, and once more faced the cameras. He felt a sudden swell of emotion as he went on.

"A short time ago, our navy's Sixth Fleet landed in the city of Tripoli, which, as the capital of Libya, has been a nucleus of international terrorist activity for far too many years."

He transposed the middle vowel and consonant of the subject of the sentence—it came out as *nookie-less* instead of *nuke-lee-us*, but Americans had heard the same gaffe a thousand times already and no one laughed anymore.

"We are now in complete control of Tripoli," he went on. "The Libyan dictator, Mohammad al-Sharq, took his own life while in the custody of our military forces, which have liberated the North African country that this tyrant has held in the grip of terror for a very long time.

"The United States decided to take this action because of links between Libya's leader and terrorists who recently hijacked the cruise liner *King Albert III*, and who we believe also attempted to engineer nuclear attacks on the United States with the assistance and aid of the tyrant in Tripoli.

"This military action, coupled with the bilateral agreements to withdraw European Defense Force and New Soviet Union troops from the front lines in the southern Caucasus, just negotiated by special presidential envoy Warren Hunnicutt, means that Americans from sea to shining sea can now draw breath more easily in the hopes of a tomorrow that is free from the threat of terrorism and war.

"My fellow Americans, I believe that we should now all give thanks for the freedoms—"

For millions of viewers of the president's speech, those words were the last they heard as their screens were suddenly filled with frenzied video static and the harsh electronic crackle of powerful digital jamming.

When the static cleared, the president's face was no more than a blurred background silhouette. A new visage had appeared in stark close-up, bold and distinct.

It was a face many had seen before and which, since the coordinated terrorist attacks on the United States that came to be known as Strike Day, had never been seen again. It was the face of a man whom Americans had for a long time, and gratefully, considered dead.

It was the sinister, aquiline face of a cold-blooded mass murderer and religious lunatic bent on the destruction of the United States.

It was the face of the terrorist chieftain who called himself the Mahdi.

Don't miss the page-turning
suspense, intriguing characters,
and unstoppable action that keep
readers coming back for more from
these bestselling authors...

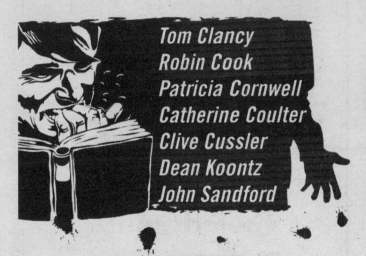

Tom Clancy
Robin Cook
Patricia Cornwell
Catherine Coulter
Clive Cussler
Dean Koontz
John Sandford

Your favorite thrillers
and suspense novels
come from Berkley.

penguin.com